MISTRESS OF MISFORTUNE

DREDTHORNE HALL BOOK 1

HAZEL HUNTER

Hazel loves hearing from readers!
You can contact her at the links below.

Website: hazelhunter.com

Facebook:
business.facebook.com/HazelHunterAuthor

Newsletter: HazelHunter.com/news

I send newsletters with details on new releases, special offers, and other bits of news related to my writing. You can sign up here!

*D*riving to Dredthorne Hall had not been Miss Meredith Starling's original intention when she had set out from the house that afternoon. In the rig she carried two baskets of fine, ripe apricots to be delivered to the village, along with messages from her mother.

"Tell the sisters Brexley these should do very well for jam," Lady Helena Starling had said from the morning room chaise lounge she occupied most of each day. "But they must use them before Sunday or they will surely go rotten. Pray do not put the second basket into the vicar's hands, for I know Mr. Branwen will eat too many and make himself sick again. You may take them to his wife directly, for she will know where to best conceal them until she can make them into tarts. You are certain that you do not wish Percival to accompany you?"

"I am, Mama." Meredith smiled to conceal her annoyance. "Now rest, and I will be back in time for tea."

As she drove from her parent's modest estate Meredith still brooded over the necessity to insist she could manage the simple errand alone. Her mother often begged Captain Percival Starling to play her escort, something that mortified Meredith. She was very fond of her cousin, but she certainly didn't require him to tag along after her everywhere. Meredith had already made peace with the misfortune that plagued her life; why couldn't her mother?

Agitation kindled a rare flash of rebellion, and when Meredith reached the crossroads she turned the rig in the opposite direction from the village. She needed more time to sort out her thoughts before she braced the vicar and the Sisters Brexley. Surely it would do no harm to enjoy the crisp air and golden sunlight by herself; anyone would agree that it was the perfect day for a ride through the country.

You mean another ride past The House, her conscience chided.

Meredith would never admit it to another soul, but long ago she had formed a secret fascination for Dredthorne Hall. Built over a century past by Emerson Thorne, an immensely wealthy gentleman with a scandalous affection for French chateaus, the old house stood like a brooding bastion of hauteur on a high hill overlooking the sprawling lands and forests belonging to the estate. Compared to the other country manors neighboring the village it seemed wholly out of place. Yet while many disdained Dredthorne's elegantly shabby façade, unfashionable staircase towers and overgrown terraced gardens, Meredith had always felt a strange affinity with the house.

No other young ladies of her acquaintance shared her interest, but that had more to do with the Thorne family curse.

The dark, wicked legends about Dredthorne Hall abounded, of course. Like all small villages, Renwick had stalwart gossips who collected such scandalous lore to discuss in avid murmurs over afternoon tea. Some insisted that the original owner had died of a broken heart on the very day the house was finished (Meredith's father claimed that tale a ridiculous fiction, as church records plainly showed Mr. Thorne had occupied the house for over a decade before succumbing to a prolonged illness.) Several servants who had abruptly left their positions at the estate claimed ghosts wandered wailing through the halls at night (Meredith's mother insisted this was petty revenge on their part for being dismissed for various infractions.) Even more fantastic tales of Dredthorne's lost treasures and ferocious monsters frequently circulated, all of which came without a mention of witnesses or a shred of proof.

The most persistent and ominous rumor had always been the Thorne family curse. According to the local tell-tales, every master of Dredthorne was doomed to fall in love with a lady who spent a night in the house. This then cursed not the gentleman but the lady, for anyone who dared to become the mistress of

Dredthorne Hall inevitably came to a swift, horrible end.

"Some go mad and must be locked away, poor dears," Meredith's aunt insisted. "Others vanish, never to be seen again. But most of the poor ladies are found dead in that wretched house, always within a few months of the wedding. Slain by their evil husbands, I daresay."

While every gossip in the village repeated this nonsense as absolute fact, Meredith found it almost laughable. The masters of Dredthorne had likely been no more cursed or evil than any fabulous wealthy gentlemen. She felt sure such privileged Londoners viewed the country as a place of respite, not residence.

No Thorne had even bothered to visit Dredthorne Hall for the last fifty years, until the new heir had arrived a month past.

As for that mysterious gentleman being cursed to love only a woman who spent the night alone in his house, to Meredith that seemed an utter Banbury tale. He certainly would be obliged to marry such a lady – but only if he wished to avoid ruining her reputation and permanently incurring the wrath of her family. She imagined honor-bound marriages did take place regularly in London, where society was fast, immense, and said to thrive on such intrigues, but they simply didn't happen here.

In Renwick the modest social calendar moved at a crawl. Every family knew each other, and closely watched over every unmarried daughter until her most advantageous match could be arranged. Indeed, a young lady could not wear a new bonnet to church without becoming the talk of the village.

"Not that I'll ever marry, Bessie," Meredith told her horse as she tugged on the reins to slow the rig. "Perhaps if I remind Mama of that, she will not mind so much letting me out of our house."

Bessie's bridle jingled as she shook her head and snorted.

As her elderly parents' primary source of companionship Meredith devoted much of her time to them. Being a good and attentive daughter was the only way she could show her gratitude for the endless trouble her misfortunes had caused them. Yet as the years passed, and all of her friends married and started their families, her own loneliness grew.

Unhappily that, like Meredith's luck, would never change.

Ahead of the rig the road smoothed out and forked off into the first of the four drives traversing the grounds of Dredthorne Hall. On each side of the long-bricked drive twin stately lions carved from moss-mottled Italian marble sat atop Doric-styled pedestal columns to which iron gates had once been attached. They had likely been removed some time in the past by a tenant seeking more ready access to the estate, and since never replaced.

"Good morning, Augustus, Tiberius," Meredith murmured, ducking her head in mock deference as she passed them. As a girl she'd been a little afraid of the fierce-faced beasts, for it had seemed as if they had glared directly down at her. Once she had secretly named them, however, they seemed far less imposing.

She then looked up at The House (for Meredith could not think of it as anything less grand); which sat like an aging beauty in her best finery atop that immaculate hill, waiting for a beau that would never come.

A veteran of many such rides, Bessie slowed on her own while Meredith beheld Dredthorne's expansive north façade. Soft grey slate roofs capped the mellow buff stone and brick of the house, which flanked by its unusual staircase towers on either end presented to the eye like a small castle. Constructed of towering, intricately-sculpted marble panels depicting life-sized warrior angels, the front vestibule had an unearthly quality more like a gateway to another world than an entrance to a dwelling. Sadly, time had weathered the exterior, adding cracks and pitting to nearly all of the house's features, but for Meredith that added to its air of mystery. In the sunlight the house took on a faint glow that obscured most of the obvious decay, making it shimmer against the horizon.

How could anyone believe such a lovely place to be dark or wicked?

Meredith tugged Bessie to a stop, and regarded the house for a long moment before she allowed herself a single, unhappy sigh. She would have given anything to see the inside, but her parents were hardly sociable. She could not recall the last time they had gone out to call on their neighbors; they preferred to host friends at their home. Aside from seeing to the occasional errand, and attending church services on Sunday, Meredith also rarely went anywhere. That was not likely to change, either, thanks to Dredthorne's new master, the reclusive Colonel Alistair Thorne.

The ladies of the village had much to say about the colonel, as they had grown seriously displeased with him.

"We were so looking forward to welcoming the colonel into our society," Lady Hardiwick had told Meredith's mother when she came with several of her friends for tea. "But he will not have us. He accepts none of our invitations, and has his man turn away every caller at the door."

"Perhaps he is ill, my lady, and cannot stand the company as yet," the vicar's wife, Mrs. Branwen, suggested with her usual cautious diffidence. "Mr. Branwen mentioned that he is just returned from serving in India."

Her ladyship sniffed. "Our dear Gerald is come back to us this very month on injury leave, with his bad leg still paining him terribly. Yet compared to the colonel, my son is the toast of the town."

"Thorne is likely still occupied with settling his domestics," Meredith's mother said, and then frowned. "Do you know, I have heard that he brought them with him from India. All of them men."

"Heathens in turbans, I was told," Lady Hardiwick said, her expression darkening. "They speak no English and dress very oddly. I think it disgusting."

"Surely not," Mrs. Branwen said. "It is an act of charity to bring them here, and give them work."

"That is his problem," Lady Starling told her. "A single man can never manage a household with any degree of competence, and he has the added misfortune of overrunning his with foreigners. No wonder he cannot get on. I wager he will very soon be of a mind to be more sociable, if only to find a wife."

"Well, he will not have my Prudence," Lady Hardiwick stated flatly. "I don't care how rich he is, you know what they say about ladies who marry Thorne men. And I refuse to have such a strange, disagreeable fellow as my son-in-law."

Meredith recalled how tightly she had pressed her lips together after that remark. Prudence Hardiwick was five years her senior, and while passably attractive had no personality. Whenever a man spoke to her, she giggled incessantly, a habit she had cultivated sometime during her three seasons in London. No gentleman had ever offered for her, much to no one's surprise and her mother's great displeasure.

These days Prudence spent most of her time in the company of her friends as they shopped, gossiped and ogled any member of the militia unfortunate enough to cross their path. No doubt being presented to Colonel Thorne would send Prudence into mirthful paroxysms, but Meredith imagined the simpering lady would have little appeal for such a traveled veteran.

"I expect I have now dashed your hopes, Meredith," Lady Hardiwick said, and patted her hand. "But you are the better for it. No young lady should saddle herself with an unmannerly husband, no matter how desperate her situation."

"Indeed." Meredith smiled as she imagined pouring the rest of her tea over her ladyship's feathered bonnet. "You are very kind to say so, ma'am."

"My poor darling girl." Lady Starling released a long sigh. "Her father and I cannot work out why she must suffer so terribly, for she is everything sweetness," she said, as if her daughter wasn't in the room.

"I am not suffering, Mama," Meredith said quietly. "I always mend."

Lady Starling ignored her to address the vicar's wife. "I live for the day that the good Lord hears my prayers, Deidre, and removes this terrible burden from her."

"I am sure He will, my lady." Mrs. Branwen gave Meredith a sympathetic look. "You seem quite recovered from that dreadful fall you had last month, my dear."

Meredith forced a smile. "I am, ma'am, thank you."

Now, sitting outside Dredthorne, Meredith could understand why the colonel had refused to have anything to do with his neighbors. Country villages were filled with the hopeful and often conniving parents of unmarried daughters; he must have known he'd be a target of matrimonial machinations from the moment he moved into the house. Still, it was odd that he had refused to allow *any* callers. The vicar would have been among the first to attempt to welcome him, and no one ever turned away the perennially ebullient Mr. Branwen.

Perhaps he is too unwell to accept visitors. Whenever Meredith's bad luck resulted in an injury she wanted to do nothing but stay in her room and be left alone until the pain eased. A soldier like the colonel would understand how difficult it was to put on a brave face when one felt wretched.

"Out of the way!"

The shout wrenched Meredith from her thoughts, and she glanced over her shoulder to see a farmer with a heavily-laden cart barreling straight at her. Quickly she slapped Bessie's rump with the reins, and drove the rig to one side to allow him past. As soon as he did, Bessie whinnied angrily and started off after him.

"Whoa, girl, whoa," Meredith called out, tugging desperately on the reins. Bessie screeched and reared, something cracked, and the rig suddenly tipped to one side, hurling Meredith from her seat.

She landed on the roadside painfully, crying out as her arm twisted under her, and cowering when the rig crashed on its side not a handspan from her face. Clods of dirt from the impact pelted her; she saw Bessie's legs churning as the spooked horse desperately tried to free herself from the overturned rig.

Meredith rolled over and hissed as her wrist blazed with pain; she cradled it against her breast and used her uninjured arm to push herself up. Once on her feet she staggered to the horse and tried to catch her bridle, but Bessie was too quick for her.

"Stand back," a deep male voice said, and a fair-haired man with a severe expression appeared on the other side of the horse, his large hands reaching for the bridle and reins. "I have her."

Meredith nodded and staggered backward, nearly falling down again before she caught herself. The speed and remarkable calm with which the man caught, quieted and detached Bessie from the rig made her heave a sigh of relief; she couldn't have done the same with only one functioning arm. "Thank you, sir. I don't know what I would have done without your help."

"You could have been trampled, you foolish girl." The man looked across Bessie's broad back, stared at her arm and then at her face, the anger in his steel-gray eyes fading. "You're hurt."

"I fell on my arm. It's nothing." Meredith saw the world tilt and then she was looking at it sideways through a fringe of grass. As the stern-faced stranger knelt before her, she reached out to him.

"I'm so sorry," she murmured as he took her hand in his. "I only meant to look at the house for a moment."

Colonel Alistair Thorne gazed down at the young woman. Her pale face had gone still, and her slim cold hand lay limp between his. She was not indulging in a fit of vapors but had fainted from genuine shock or worse. As he gathered her into his arms, he took another look at the broken rig and the mare now placidly cropping grass beside it. It seemed obvious that the horse had spooked and reared, causing the rig to crash on its side.

"Master." Harshad, his steward and a former officer in the army of India, appeared at his side. His dark eyes widened as he beheld the woman. "Who is this?"

"I haven't a bloody clue. I must use your cart." He stood and nodded toward the mare. "Take the horse to the stables and ask Kshantu to have a look at her. Tell him she's lost a shoe."

Harshad gave him a quick bow and went to attend to the mare. Alistair carried the young woman across the road and through the lionsgate to the cart Harshad had left on the drive. After carefully placing her in the back with the sacks of feed his steward had bought in town, he climbed up and drove the cart horses to the front of the house.

Alistair discovered his passenger stirring as he lifted her out of the cart and took her inside the house. The sepoys Harshad has trained to serve as his footmen remained at their posts, but both gave the young woman wary looks. Since Alistair had taken up residence at Dredthorne no outsider had crossed the threshold, and he had resolved to keep it that way.

"I beg your pardon," a soft voice said, and Alistair looked down into jade-colored eyes. "Who are you, and where am I?"

"Colonel Alistair Thorne, at your service." He carried her into his morning room, and carefully placed her in his favorite armchair. As he straightened and took a step back to give her a polite bow, he felt the inexplicable urge to scoop her up and hold her again. "You are at my home, Dredthorne Hall."

"Dredthorne? But I was only just…" The young woman went very still. "Bessie." She sat up and regarded him with visible panic. "My rig… I had an accident, and my horse–"

"She lost a shoe, but I believe otherwise she is fine," Alistair assured her. "I had my steward take her to my stablemaster. He will attend her."

"Thank you, sir." She sank back, a little color returning to her cheeks. "I feel so dreadful for imposing on you like this. If you will give me a few moments to collect myself, I will leave you in peace."

"You are not going anywhere like that, young woman." He nodded at her injured limb. "Do I have your permission to examine the arm?"

"You need not, sir," she said quickly. "I think it is only a bad wrench."

"Oh, you are a doctor?" he asked, pretending surprise. "That is quite providential. My right shoulder has been paining me of late. Perhaps, when you are recovered, you would be good enough to look at it?"

"You know I am not a doctor," she chided. "If my arm were broken, it should hurt a great deal more than it does."

The fact that she would know such a thing troubled Alistair, and he knelt beside the chair.

"What is your name?" When she hesitated, he added, "I know it is not proper to ask so directly, but I must call you something other than 'young woman'."

"Of course, forgive me. I am Miss Meredith Starling." She offered him her good hand. "I am happy to make your acquaintance, Colonel."

"The pleasure is mine." He clasped her hand briefly. "Now, Miss Starling, please allow me to ascertain that your arm is not seriously injured. Broken bones are nothing to trifle with, and I have much experience with such injuries from my years in the Army."

She gave a reluctant nod and winced as she held out her arm.

Alistair supported the limb with one hand and carefully felt along the length of it with the other. She caught her breath when he touched her wrist but made no other sound. He then bent the limb up from the elbow to establish her range of function, at which point he saw the red stain on the underside of her sleeve.

"It is not broken, but your wrist is badly sprained, and you are bleeding," he said, gently lowering her arm. "I will send to the village for the doctor."

"He is not there," she told him. "Doctor Mallory's father fell ill, and he traveled to

London last week to visit him. But he should return by week-end."

That left Alistair with no choice. "Then with your permission, I will cut open your sleeve and treat the wound."

She paled but nodded quickly.

"I must fetch my medical case." He stood. "Do not move from this chair while I am gone."

* * *

MEREDITH MAINTAINED her façade of serenity until the colonel left the room, at which point she collapsed back against the chair with a groan. The bad luck of the rig accident didn't surprise her, but she had never fainted in such a ridiculous fashion. Waking up to find herself the guest of the stern-face colonel had completely bewildered her, too. As reclusive as he was, why would he trouble himself to look after a stranger who had been silly enough to ditch her rig by the road?

He is simply being polite, Meredith thought. *Though he may be terse and abrupt, he is still a gentleman.*

While the means had been rather drastic, her dearest wish to see the inside of the house had been granted. It was more beautiful than she had ever imagined. The room in which the colonel had brought her appeared to be a morning salon, abundantly furnished with several chairs, lounges and one particularly sumptuous velvet and whitewood settee. In contrast to their surroundings everything looked new, suggesting the colonel had brought them with him to Dredthorne. The soft silvery fabrics went well with the Grecian design of the faded embossed wallpapers, and the old yet intricate Persian rugs. Meredith thought the rough gray quarry stone used to frame the fireplace exceptionally suitable, given the portrait of the iron-haired gentleman hanging above it.

The style of that painting, and the fact that its subject wore a jacket that had been fashionable a century past, made Meredith wonder if she was looking upon the original owner of Dredthorne. His long face and lantern-shaped jaw seemed quite severe, but the artist had captured something softer in his eyes. Sorrow, perhaps, or an intense longing.

"You have a delightful home, sir," she murmured, and then jumped a little as Colonel Thorne came in with a large leather case under his arm and a tea tray in his hands. On the tray was not the makings of any tea, but some folded linen, a pair of shears and a rather large open decanter of dark amber liquid. "Pray, what are those spirits for, Colonel?"

"You," he said as he set down the case and tray, and then saw her face. "More precisely, your arm, Miss Starling. Untreated wounds can easily fester."

"Yes, of course." She heard a booming sound and the rattling of windows, which had grown puzzlingly dark. "Oh my, have the French invaded Renwick?"

"Lightning. A very large storm has blown in," the colonel said as he picked up the shears, and paused as a muffled drumming sound filled the room. "And there is the rain."

Meredith watched as he took the shears to her sleeve and carefully cut it apart to a few inches above her elbow before snipping it away entirely. As she turned her wrist she grimaced; her fall had left a large, unsightly graze on the underside of her forearm. "Doctor Mallory always uses coal tar soap for such things."

"Soap is rarely found on the battlefield," the colonel said as he cradled her arm with the folded linen and picked up the decanter. "But liquor can always be had wherever men fight." He met her gaze. "This will burn, my dear, but only for a few moments. Brace yourself."

Meredith felt herself blushing at his casual endearment and quickly nodded, biting her lip as he poured the spirits over the wound. The pain she managed as always by concentrating on her breathing to keep it slow and deep.

Thorne set down the decanter and blotted the excess from the wound before examining it closely. "I do not see any dirt or debris lingering. I will bandage it now."

"Thank you, sir," she said, feeling despite her efforts a little light-headed, and then cringed as a huge bang exploded outside the house. "This storm must be very bad."

"It will likely turn the roads to rivers."

He removed from the leather case a roll of white, loosely-woven cloth, which he used to dress the wound. He then took out what appeared to be half a leather glove encircled by a number of narrow, buckled straps.

"This will allow the sprain to better heal," he said as he fitted the odd glove over her hand. Once he tightened the buckled straps around her wrist Meredith found that she could wriggle her fingers but not move her hand at all.

"I think Doctor Mallory would be very interested in this," she told him. "He resorts to wood slats and cloth ties to immobilize injured parts, and they are quite awkward. They also itch terribly."

Thorne sat back on his haunches and regarded her with a frown. "Exactly how often have you injured yourself, Miss Starling?"

"More than I should," she admitted, and forced a smile. "Now I have imposed on you too much for even the most generous of good Samaritans. If you would be so kind as to have my rig brought up, I will trespass on your kindness no longer."

"The roads are flooding, and your rig is

in pieces, Miss Starling," he said bluntly. "You have had a very bad shock and should not be moved. Once the storm passes I will send word to your parents of your accident, but you are not leaving."

$\mathcal{I}$t took a moment for Meredith to set aside her dismay and respond to Alistair Thorne's alarming declaration. "Thank you, sir, but I cannot linger."

The colonel's eyebrows arched. "You have a pressing appointment elsewhere?"

"I intended to deliver apricots to some of our acquaintances in the village, but that will be impossible in the storm." That he didn't recognize the impropriety of their situation seemed clear, but pointing that out would be unmannerly. "My mother warned me to stay away from Dredthorne Hall, so I should not even be here. When night falls and I do not return, she and my father will become frantic."

"I could allow you to return home, I

suppose," Thorne said, and outside lighting struck again, causing the opaque window panes to rattle. "My carriage is presently at the wheelwright for repairs, but there is the cart. The horse may not mind a one-armed driver."

And now he was laughing at her. "I am happy to walk," Meredith assured him.

"On foot I expect it would take you perhaps an hour, provided you are not swept away by a sudden torrent." The hard line of his mouth curved. "Are you a good walker in a flood, Miss Starling?"

"No one is, Colonel." As accustomed as she was to her misfortunes, it seemed very unfair that he should be entertained by them. "I am glad that you find my situation diverting."

"The estate agent mentioned how notorious Dredthorne Hall has become with the locals." Thorne said. "That you *survived* a night under my roof should make you the heroine of the season."

So, he knew about the curse, Meredith thought. He seemed indifferent to the rumors, which made her feel a little easier. As for her own predicament, she would simply tell her mother that she had taken refuge in the village, and no one would ever be the wiser.

"The storm should not last. They never do here," Meredith said, but when she saw him untying his cravat she went still. "Sir?"

"Calm yourself. It is the only silk I have at hand." Once he unwrapped the snowy length from his strong throat, Thorne folded it in half and held it diagonally across the front of his jacket. "It will serve as a comfortable sling for your arm."

"Yes, that would be helpful." Meredith sat forward as he draped her neck with the soft, thin fabric and cradled her arm with it. From the silk she could feel the heat of the colonel's body, and smelled a trace of some dark, spicy scent she could not identify. She had never been so near a stranger, and the thudding of her heart perplexed her.

Why in Heaven's name did she wish nothing more than to move even closer to him?

"You should rest before luncheon." Thorne straightened and offered her his hand. "Allow me to escort you to one of the guest rooms."

"Thank you, Colonel." Meredith's fingers trembled as she gripped his and rose slowly. Her head felt as wobbly as her knees, but when he tucked her arm securely in his she steadied. "You are everything kindness."

Thorne gave her an odd look. "Hardly."

She tried not to gawk about her as Thorne guided her out of the morning room and into the reception hall, but the timeworn beauty of Dredthorne could not be ignored. Above her head soaring ceilings adorned with paintings of cherubs and angels soared, framed by gilded alabaster carvings so intricate they appeared to be constructed of golden lace. Even the copious amount of ancient abandoned spider webs festooning them could not obscure their artful appeal. Dusty paintings occupied every wall in sight, in clever arrangements that captured the eye and invited longer contemplation. Although entirely out of fashion with the current trend of sculpture salons, the free-standing statues that appeared in random spots seemed perfectly placed, and were often flanked by over-large floor vases containing small trees and foliage. Unhappily all of the plants had died long ago.

Why didn't the colonel have fresh flowers brought in to provide some color and fragrance to the gloomy hall? Surely there was plenty to be had from the gardens.

How presumptuous, her conscience chided. *Not an hour under his roof, and you've already made yourself mistress of the house.*

The staircase to which Thorne led Meredith flowed up from the scarred, darkened walnut floors like a long, elegant arm gesturing toward the clouds. Once more her secret desire to climb one of Dredthorne's staircase towers returned to her, but she couldn't ask to traipse across the house for such a whim. She paused to admire the gray-shot white marble steps, which even with the edge chipping and cracks invoked a sense of stepping onto clouds.

"You've noticed the abundance of fripperies my ancestors installed," the colonel said as they proceeded up the staircase. "They quite overrun the place."

His masculine contempt made her hide

a smile. "The first Mr. Thorne was said to be quite enamored with all things French."

"A regrettable inclination," Thorne said. "Yet thanks to the Regent it remains an enduring craze in London. I feel fortunate not to have a pink and white writing table in my study."

"I have heard India described as most exotic," she said, hoping he would not think her over-curious. "Is it very different from England?"

"Indeed, for their ways are decidedly unlike ours," he told her. "The natives consider all animals holy. They regard cows as most sacred, and never use them for meat. They paint and adorn the beasts and permit them to freely roam."

"How exceptional." Meredith supposed such a thing would appall most beef-loving Englishmen, but she thought the practice rather endearing. "Is it true that they travel by elephant?"

"They do. They also worship the beasts." His jaw tightened. "As well as monkeys and snakes."

Once on the second-floor landing the colonel guided her to a spacious guest room at the back of the house. Meredith halted outside the threshold as she took in the antique white furnishings and faded green and floral decor. From the traces of paint that remained on the walls they had once portrayed a flower-speckled meadow beneath blues skies with golden clouds. The chamber had been recently cleaned and dusted, and the linens replaced. Yet everything she saw suggested that, like the rest of the house, no one had slept here for at least fifty years.

Such a pity, she thought, and then regarded her host, whose expression seemed impatient. "I have kept you too long. Thank you again, Colonel."

He inclined his head. "Rest, and we will talk again at luncheon."

* * *

WITH RELUCTANCE THORNE left Meredith and returned downstairs to his study. The stack of letters on his desk awaiting his response did not interest him, for he knew they were more of the same entreaties from his former Army comrades in India. Even the General himself had written, demanding to know why he had resigned his commission.

You have been the most effective field officer under my command, Jarvis had penned in his own bold, slashing hand. *You must know that I cannot replace you. If you desire a promotion, you shall have it. If it is a question of finances, they will be managed. You have but to name your terms, and I will attend to them personally.*

Jarvis did not exaggerate or make false promises; Thorne could ask for virtually anything, even his own elephant, and the General would have it waiting for him on the docks in Mumbai. Yet he could not return, for he remained unfit to serve king and country.

A throat cleared behind him, and he glanced over his shoulder at Harshad. "What of the mare?"

"She is well, Master. The stablemaster found nothing amiss," his steward said. "He has replaced the shoe and watered and fed her."

Thorne imagined that news would relieve his guest. "The young lady has injured her arm, and with the storm she must stay the night. I have put her in that green guest room. Advise Cook there will be two for the meals." He saw Harshad's expression. "What is it?"

"Kshantu heard a dog howling in the night," Harshad said. "It means–"

"Death is coming." Thorne did not subscribe to such superstitions, but while in India he had learned to respect how seriously his native troops attended to them. "Does he mean to string lemons and chilies over the doors?"

Harshad grimaced. "That he is has already attended to, Master. But he feels the rig crashing out on the road was no accident. Someone has beset the girl with the evil eye."

"We do not curse ladies in England, Harshad." Even as he said that, Thorne felt again that something seemed very odd about Meredith Starling's mishap. Could she have contrived it in order to gain admittance to the house? She did seem particularly enchanted by Dredthorne. "Once the rain stops bring her rig into the barn. While you're there please assure

Kshantu that this is all simply an unhappy coincidence."

"As you say, Master." His steward bowed and retreated from the room.

Thorne went to the north-faced window of his study, and looked out through the murky panes at the drive. As soon as the weather cleared he would have to return Miss Starling to her family, and endure the accusations they would hurl. Any attempt to bully him into offering for their daughter, however, was doomed to fail.

Even before he had been beset by his affliction, marriage had never tempted him.

Thorne had spent his childhood watching his ill-suited parents grow apart. His mother despised the port towns in which they had lived while his father was off at sea, and kept to her rooms most of her life. His father in turn felt contempt for his wife's petulant inability to perform even some of her duties as a mother. A succession of nannies had raised Alistair until he was of age to be sent away to school.

Nor had there been any choice of

professions for the only son of Captain Thomas Thorne; once his studies had ended his father had promptly begun making arrangements for his entry into the Navy. But Alistair had never cared for the sea, and preempted the captain's machinations by taking a commission in the Army.

The only act of outright defiance Alistair had ever committed had been enough to completely sever his relationship with his father. Thomas Thorne had immediately declared him disowned, and had never spoken to him again.

Alistair tried to keep in contact with his mother by writing to her, but never received a single reply. He imagined the captain had also seen to that by destroying the letters or forbidding his wife to respond. In time he had abandoned writing, and from then on considered himself as good as an orphan.

Rumor mills and grapevines riddled the military, and it was through the latter that Alistair learned his parents had drowned when a pleasure boat they had chartered sank off the coast of Spain. Although

Thorne had not seen his family in more than a decade, their loss ended all hope of someday reconciling with them.

He almost threw away the letter that came from Thomas's attorney. Yet when he read that the captain had not, in fact, legally disowned him, grief over losing his parents twice had finally made him weep.

As the sole heir of Thomas's estate, Alistair discovered he was suddenly and enormously wealthy, thanks to his father's bewildering legacy. Throughout his life he could not recall the captain ever once mentioning his family, their wealth or Dredthorne Hall. Wherever his father had left them, Alistair and his mother had lived comfortably but simply in unpretentious houses staffed by only a few servants.

Major Nigel Robbins, his closest friend in the regiment, had come upon him just after the letter arrived. "I say, Alistair, you look dreadful. Have you been eating the native swill again?"

Without a word he'd handed the letter to his friend, whose eyes widened as he read through the pages.

"Good God, man. You are become

Croesus." Nigel set down the letter and dropped into the camp chair beside him. "What will you do now that your late father has enabled you to purchase any middling-size country on the planet?"

"I defied the Captain when I joined the Army, and he never forgave me for it. I daresay he despised me until the day he died, and drowned my mother with him." Alistair took up the letter, held one corner to his tent lamp until it caught fire, and dropped it in his washing basin to watch it burn. "I want no part of it."

"I understand your sentiments completely," Nigel said solemnly. "Will you give it to me, then? I should dearly like the means with which to buy most of England."

His friend had gotten him to laugh on that dreadful day, and many more after it, Alistair remembered. When Nigel had been killed during an uprising Alistair had ignored his own injuries to carry his friend from the battlefield. He remembered little of what followed; later he was told he collapsed outside the casualty tents, still clutching his dead friend. Alistair spent the next weeks in hospital, barely clinging to life himself. Yet while in time his bodily wounds healed, he discovered that the grisly battle had robbed him of more than the best of friends. Now he suspected his affliction a punishment that, like his guilt, would only end when his life did.

I should have died in Nigel's place.

Several thumps on the ceiling above Thorne dragged him out of his brooding thoughts. The green guest room lay directly above his study, which meant Miss Starling was the source of the noise. "What the devil is she doing up there? Rearranging the…"

Thorne fell silent as an image of Meredith Starling's face just before she had fallen over in the grass flashed through his mind. Such violent accidents often inflicted multiple injuries, particularly when a body was hurled through the air to the ground.

He had checked her arm thoroughly, but he hadn't once considered that she might have struck her head as well. "Damn me."

Thorne ran for the stairs.

* * *

MEREDITH LAY ON THE MATTED, faded

green rug that she guessed had once resembled grass. Its aged fibers crunched beneath her slight weight with every move, but it had cushioned her landing, and spared her hurt arm more damage. What stung was the fact that her skirts had tangled around her legs like swaddling, constricting their movement entirely. With only one arm functioning she then discovered she could not rise under her own power.

"I will simply be content to wait here," she told the old rug with as much cheer as she could summon. "Someone should come along eventually."

Behind her the door to the room flung open, and a familiar voice uttered a scalding oath.

"Colonel Thorne." She turned her head and lifted her chin to smile at him. "Might I ask for your help again?"

He knelt beside her. "Did you faint?"

"No, sir. I slipped." As he eased her over onto her back, she stared up at the ceiling and tried to think of how she might distract him from this new evidence of her ungainliness. "I had not noticed the lovely painting up there. Such pretty clouds. Oh, forgive me, I think those are water marks."

"I will take your word for it." Thorne worked his hand beneath her shoulders and carefully raised her to a sitting position. "I should not have left you alone."

"The fault is mine, Colonel," she assured him. "I should not have been traipsing about in my condition."

The colonel's eyes looked bluer now. Tiny streaks of white in the irises made them seem lighter than they were. It made Meredith wonder if they changed color, as her own sometimes seemed to do. She found herself breathing in his enthralling scent, which made her head spin as wildly as a weather vane in high wind. This was why the young ladies in the village giggled so madly whenever young men came near. No gentleman of her acquaintance had ever come so close to Meredith, but with her reputation doubtless they regarded proximity to her as more of a personal hazard.

"Are you hurt, Miss Starling?"

His sharp inquiry made her realize how shamelessly she had been gawking at him.

"I'm clumsy but unharmed, sir." She felt the coils of her hair slipping down her nape and grimaced. "Although my hair pins seem to have abandoned me."

"I should examine your head," he said, waiting for her nod before he ran his fingers over her head. "When you were thrown from the rig, did you strike it?"

"No, I landed on my side." She winced as his fingers touched a sore spot at the very back of her skull. "Ouch. Perhaps I am mistaken."

"Be still." He moved around her and parted her hair.

As Thorne went about inspecting her head the lamp illuminated his face, revealing the faint shadows beneath his eyes. She'd assumed the set of his features reflected a natural sternness, but now she saw the signs of true weariness. He'd shown no sign of injury or illness, which made her wonder why he looked so tired.

"You have a small lump here," he said, his breath stirring the fine hairs on her nape.

She suppressed a shiver of reaction. "I did lose my balance fall back against the bed frame, and then pitched forward. I am prone to such inelegant– Oh."

Thorne ignored her gasp as he picked her up in his arms and carried her over to the bed. "I'll have the damned rug ripped out and burned."

His language did not shock Meredith as much as his anger. As he lowered her atop the coverlet, she thought of how she sometimes teased her father out of a dour mood.

"Do you mean to do the same with my shoes and stockings? For then I would have to return barefoot, which would give my mother the hysterics. If the rest does not," she added as he bent over her.

His expression remained bleak. "I will never tell your mother." He took off her shoes and dropped them on the floor before he scowled. "What happened here?"

"An unhappy gift from my seventh birthday." Meredith couldn't quite straighten that foot, and saw that the old scars showed through a tear in her worn stocking. "I've always been somewhat scatter-brained, and stepped into a poacher's trap. I could not free myself, so there I stayed for the afternoon."

Thorne stroked his thumb over the section of stocking covering the raised marks. "You must have been terrified."

The way he touched her made Meredith's toes curl. "At the time I was playing hound and fox with my cousin in the woods. I was the fox. He assumed I'd found an excellent hiding place, but happily in time he found me."

Thorne straightened. "I will prepare a poultice for your head, and fetch a tray for you. While I am gone you are not to move from this bed, is that understood?"

"I will not twitch an eyelid, Colonel," she assured him.

A minute after her host departed Meredith promptly broke her promise and sat up. Carefully she felt the lump at the back of her head, and then eyed her reflection in the mottled mirror across from the bed. "Don't look at me like that. I told him what a turnip-head I am."

The other Meredith glowered back at her in silent agreement.

She closed her eyes and eased back

against the pillows. Making a list of her present regrets would likely take hours, but she couldn't resist. How could she have been so hapless as to have *two* accidents in a single morning? Would this appalling weather abate before nightfall? What must Colonel Thorne think of her now? Never had Meredith made such a spectacle of herself. And why in Heaven's name hadn't she worn her new stockings today?

You want to stay at Dredthorne, her conscience scolded her. *You would happily impose yourself just so you might wallow in his attentions.*

A knock sounded, and when she called "Do come in" Thorne entered carrying another, heavily-laden tray.

Meredith regarded the large pot of tea and the heaping platter of sandwiches, cakes and fruit he carried with alarm. "Do you mean to feed a regiment, sir?"

"It is not all for you. We will have our luncheon here." He placed the tray on the bedside table, and removed from a small bowl a sodden cloth wrapped around some greenery. "My cook made up this poultice.

It may smell peculiar, but I can attest to it working wonders on a sore head."

"Have you slipped on many rugs?" she tried to joke, and then saw how the line of his mouth thinned. "Of course, you haven't."

"I became unseated during a battle, and my horse dragged me across a field," he said as he brought a chair to her bedside. "I struck my head on a stone. After the fighting I had the headache for almost a week, until my cook prepared this for me."

He didn't like to talk about India or his time in the army, Meredith realized, and wondered why. Her cousin loved to regale his friends and family with tales of his adventures while traveling abroad with his regiment.

"I am beyond fortunate to be your guest." She eyed the food on the tray. "Although the poultice may make dining somewhat awkward for me."

"I have the remedy for that." Thorne took out of his jacket pocket another length of white silk. "If you will sit up."

She pushed herself upright, and bent forward to allow him to bind the poultice to her head. As he secured the ends she caught the scent of herbs and something like boiled onion, but the damp warmth immediately eased the throbbing. His nearness, however, once more stirred her insides with excitement.

Control yourself, her conscience ordered in a voice very much like her mother's. *Ladies are calm and composed.*

"It does smell odd, but it feels very good," Meredith said, tucking a fold of the silk behind her ear. "I might wear it on my next visit to the village. Perhaps I may deflect the gossips, and start a new trend in bonnets."

"Or turbans for my servants." The colonel filled a plate with food and offered it to her. "I wager I give them the head-ache more often than not. What do your village gossips say about me?"

"You mean, besides those concerning your unwelcoming behavior, which I can now wholly refute?" She couldn't believe she'd said that, and quickly added, "I apologize. My mother tells me never to repeat such things."

Thorne gave her a narrow look. "Just as she warned you to avoid my house."

"I am a dreadful daughter." Meredith sighed. "Very well. It's said that you are an unmarried gentleman who is newly returned to England."

His brows arched. "That's all?"

"That's quite enough. There are a great many unmarried girls in the neighborhood, and very few bachelors." She held up one finger. "Our ladies do not yet know you are handsome. Once that is made common knowledge, then I fear you are in for the worst."

"I will have my steward install additional bolts on the doors." Thorne placed over her lap an artfully-carved bed tray, on which he placed a brimming cup of tea, more food and a small pitcher of cream. "I thank you for thinking me handsome, however. Perhaps I should marry you."

* * *

MEREDITH NEARLY CHOKED on her tea. "I am very flattered, Colonel, but I believe you should consider a lady more suited to your situation in life."

"Why should she not be you?" Thorne persisted.

He was laughing at her again, she suspected, so she would respond in kind. "Marriage holds no allure for me. I am a spinster in the making, you see, and quite determined to stay the course."

"I thought all young ladies, even spinsters in the making, *welcomed* the prospect of a good match," he said. "Do you mean to discourage me, or have you some other reason to avoid the altar?"

"I should not wish to trip and cosh my head on it." That frank admission made him laugh out loud, something Meredith guessed he rarely did. "If you truly seek a wife, then you have but to go out into society."

Thorne's amusement abruptly vanished. "I think not."

She watched him stand and walk over to the window. "You cannot know what you are missing, sir. I did not exaggerate about the wealth of unattached young ladies of good family around Renwick. In fact, we've become rather notorious for producing quite so many. At our assemblies there are never enough gentlemen to serve as dancing partners."

"Then you should import some younger men." He folded his hands behind him and gazed out into the rain. "I am too old for such frivolities now."

"I think not." When he eyed her, Meredith lifted her hands. "Really, Colonel, you are hardly ancient. A man of the world such as yourself would be held in very high regard by our ladies. Of course, they would have to first actually *regard* you, which they cannot do if you avoid their company."

"I have little experience in society," Thorne admitted. "In the Army there is not much opportunity for any of the decent sort. My fellow officers provided companionship, but soldiers are not inclined to play whist or chat about the temperature over tea."

Meredith sensed his excuses more polite than truthful. But what would make him wish to avoid society all together? Perhaps his military service had done something to make him feel estranged, and that was why he never cared to speak of it.

"We are not always playing cards, and we sometimes do talk about things other than the weather." She took a sip from her tea cup before she asked, "How long were you away from England?"

"Almost fourteen years. Too long to make myself agreeable to others, I should think." He glanced at her, and again she saw his weariness. "You would not understand."

"Before I crashed my rig on your road. I fell down our stairs, was attacked by a wild dog, and nearly set fire to my skirts. That was just this past month. Despite my unhappy luck I still attend assemblies, at which I do not instigate any chaos whatsoever." She gave him a cheerful smile. "If a walking calamity such as I can brave the punch bowls and card tables, sir, then surely you can."

Thorne gave her a sharp look. "You consider yourself afflicted with bad luck?"

"Undeniably so. Mr. Branwen, our vicar, says the Lord never troubles us with more burdens than we can carry," she said, and frowned at her scarred foot. "He must consider me an exceptionally capable porter."

"You show good humor in the face of adversity," he chided. "I should follow your example, but I have no acquaintances here who might be persuaded to introduce me." Thorne hesitated before he said, "Unless you would be willing to do so, Miss Starling."

Meredith's heart skipped a beat, until her sensibility squashed it. "For us to appear together would encourage certain false notions." When his expression didn't change, she said, "People would presume that you and I had formed an attachment. That would also defeat the purpose of such outings."

Thorne's mouth hitched. "Of course, we wouldn't want that."

"I could introduce you to my cousin Percival," Meredith said, ducking her head as she felt her cheeks going pink. "He's very fond of me, so he would not mind the acquaintance. He also served in the Army, so I daresay the two of you might become good friends."

"Just how fond of you *is* this cousin?" he asked bluntly.

"Oh, no, nothing like that. Percival is like an older brother to me," she assured him. "In fact, he has saved me more than once from being badly hurt during one of my misfortunes."

"He is the same cousin who rescued you from the poacher's trap?" When she nodded, he came to her side. "Very well, I will meet him. But if I am to inflict myself on Renwick society, I will do so only under one condition: that you also attend the events."

His stipulation puzzled her. "We do not have so many assemblies here that you could hope to avoid me, sir."

"Excellent." Thorne smiled. "I look forward to discussing the quirks of climate over our first game of whist."

CHAPTER 3

"Would you care for some tea, Miss Branwen?"

Lucetta looked up from her embroidery to see her sister-in-law Deidre hovering anxiously on the threshold of the parsonage's sitting room. "Thank you, no, Mrs. Branwen."

"Why do you speak so formally?" Jeffrey Branwen, the vicar of Renwick came in through the opposite door from his study to regard them both as if they'd sworn out loud. "You share the same surname, ladies. You need not use it in addressing each other."

"That is the practice of blood kin, or close friends. With all due respect, your wife is neither to me." Lucetta stabbed her needle into an unworked section within her hoop and rose to her feet. "I will go to my room."

"You'll do nothing of the sort. Since you arrived we've had barely ten minutes together to talk." Indignant now, her brother turned to his wife. "We will all have tea, my dear, and perhaps some of those lovely raspberry scones you made for breakfast."

Deidre Branwen nodded and hurried away toward the kitchen, reminding Lucetta of a chicken escaping the coop.

"I loathe fruit scones and weak tea, Jeffrey." She wandered over to the window to look at the puddles forming in his deplorable rose garden. "Go and finish writing your sermon. You may attempt again to browbeat me over the boiled beef and potatoes your bride is presently overcooking for dinner."

"I expect you are still tired after your journey," he said as he dropped into the shabby armchair by the fire. "Nevertheless, you might try to overcome your weariness to befriend my wife. You must know

Deidre wishes only to make you comfortable."

"I know that I terrify your wife, Brother, and she deeply annoys me," she informed him sharply. "Mrs. Branwen quivers whenever she addresses me. I have *eaten* braver quails."

The tip of her brother's nose turned pink; a sure sign he was in a temper. "Nonsense; she loves you already. She is your sister, as I am your brother, Lucy–"

"Do not call me that." The affectionate nickname made her hands curl into fists. "We are no longer children, sir. To you I am Lucetta, or Sister, or nothing at all."

"God in Heaven." He shot to his feet and took a step toward her. "What did that wretched man do to you?"

She considered answering his question truthfully, but thankfully, only for a moment.

"My former employer, Lord Carlton, accused me of stealing from him, and had me arrested." Even saying that man's name made her stomach curdle. "His attorney persuaded him to drop the charges against me due to lack of evidence, but his lordship dismissed me without a reference. I had no recourse but to come here and impose myself on you. Have you forgotten *everything* I wrote to you in my letter?"

"But why did this happen?" her brother pleaded.

"I had to come here, Jeffrey, or starve in the hedgerows." She tapped a finger against her cheek. "Although I might have done quite well as a pilfering vagabond."

"You are no more a criminal than I, Lucetta," he said, looking somewhat wounded now. "Whatever the circumstances, I know this is but a terrible misunderstanding that we will sort out in time."

Lucetta almost took pity on him, but the stone that had replaced her heart some months back refused to be moved. "As it happens, Jeffrey, I *am* a thief, and rather a good one. His Lordship was quite correct to toss me out into the gutter."

"I do not believe it," he said firmly. "Do you forget that I have known you all of your life? That I have seen into your good, kind heart since we were children?"

"You see only what you wish to, Brother.

I envy you that, but it does not change who I am, or what I have done. I stole very valuable property from my employer, and I do not regret it." She offered him a prim smile. "Content yourself with praying for my soul. Blackened as it is, I am sure it will benefit."

She swept past him and headed for her room at the back of the house, encountering Deidre coming out of the kitchen. "Do be aware, Mrs. Branwen, I have just freely confessed to your husband that I am a thief."

"You are?" Deidre pressed her hand to the base of her throat. "Heavens. My poor Jeffrey."

"I daresay he will survive the revelation. As this news was neither anticipated nor welcomed, however, you may wish to serve him something a little stronger than your insipid, thrice-brewed pekoe." Lucetta continued on down the hall.

Once inside the tiny servant's quarters her brother had allotted as her bedchamber, Lucetta closed the door and leaned back against it. By coming here, she had demonstrated utter, complete lunacy.

Before leaving London she had given away all of her savings, and spent her last shilling to manage the journey. She now had no means with which to extricate herself.

Where should I go?

Bitterly she thought of how only months ago her situation in life had been far more fortunate. She might have found employment instantly; she had served as governess to five of the finest families in England, and had been held in high esteem by all. She had been proud of her work with her young, privileged charges. She would still be imprinting such eager minds with all the knowledge they could hold, had it not been for her sixth and final post.

Some weeks before Lucetta had left London in disgrace, his lordship had come to her jail cell. The prosecutor had informed him that without the exact details of her crime he could not continue to keep her imprisoned, but reluctantly granted him one last interview in order to settle the matter between them.

In the end the attorney had been forced to hold his client back to prevent him from beating her with his fists. The very noble

Lord Carlton had screamed his final words to her: *Tell me where, you rat-faced bitch, or I will see you ruined.*

Lucetta had held her tongue, and the charges against her had been withdrawn. Yet upon her release she learned that his lordship had kept his final promise. Carlton had seen to it that no one in London would ever again offer her employment.

The sound of her brother and his wife's voices carrying down the hall wrenched Lucetta back to the present; it sounded as if Jeffrey were blustering and Deidre weeping. *Of course, they are. The vicar prays for felons, he doesn't keep them as guests.*

Suddenly Lucetta could not bear to spend another moment under the same roof with them, and seized her hat and cloak. Now that the storm had passed she could resume her new habit of taking a daily long walk in the countryside. The cows and horses in the fields did not care what she was called, or why she was here, or even what she had done—and they called them *dumb* animals.

She left the house through the front entrance and walked quickly down the lane until she came to the road that led to and from the village. Since she had no money she could not shop. She felt no inclination to introduce herself to people who would soon revile her, so she took the direction leading away.

Like many small towns scattered across the county, Renwick remained stolidly rural, the town a hub for a large number of farms and country properties. When her brother had finished his studies, a family friend had steered him to apply for the position of curate at Renwick. By the time the elderly vicar passed away Jeffrey had made himself so beloved by all there was no question of the living going to anyone else.

Lucetta had never envied her sibling his calling. She dutifully attended church as a matter of form, but had never felt Jeffrey's fervor for good works. She knew her brother's faith meant everything to him, but she could not share it. Now it was all she could do not to scream at him about the God he so cherished. A God that, if he truly existed, allowed horrible, vile things to happen to the most innocent of his creations.

"*Suwar ki aulad*," a man's voice uttered.

Lucetta looked ahead, and saw a man standing beside a large heap of wet, broken wood that might once have been a rig. As he wore a blue turban and carried a sword, she halted in her tracks and turned around to head in the opposite direction.

"Coward." She reversed herself again and marched forward.

* * *

HARSHAD GLANCED over at the tall, pale woman, who regarded him with interest.

"You sir," she said, "are very dark." She carried a parasol, and looked as fierce as a hawk.

"You are not," he replied.

"I am an Englishwoman. This is the only shade of skin that we are permitted at present. What were those words you uttered?"

"*Suwar ki aulad*, Miss." He thought for a moment. "In English you would say the son of a hog."

She quickly suppressed a smile as she came to stand beside him and studied the remains of the smashed rig. "This looks in sad repair. Is it yours?"

"No, Miss. I was sent by my master to collect it." He regarded the heap of shattered wood. "It was overturned this morning, but it did not look so bad as this. I think someone came during the storm and tried to move it."

"More likely they had a tantrum and smashed it to bits." The woman knelt down and studied a section of shattered wood. "This mark here came from a hammer or cudgel of some sort."

Why was this fine lady kneeling in the mud? Harshad almost tried to help her up, but then remembered his master's warning about touching any Englishwoman. "I do not know that word. What is this cudgel?"

"It is a club made of wood or metal that is used for smashing things. Heads, generally." She stood up again. "How odd that someone would take the time to do this in a storm. They must have been in quite a temper." She faced him and held out one gloved hand. "I am Lucetta Branwen, sister to Jeffrey Branwen, the vicar of Renwick. And you are…?"

"Very well, thank you. Oh, you want my name. It is Harshad Naveya." He bowed over her hand. "I serve as steward to Colonel Thorne."

"You work for the beast of Dredthorne Hall. Fascinating. How do you do, Mr. Naveya?" Lucetta bobbed.

Harshad knew enough about English customs to bow in return, but her remark made him frown. "My master is not a beast. He is a man. You are joking with me, yes?"

"Yes, I am. You speak tolerable English for, well, whatever you are." She nodded at the rig. "I should advise your master that someone has been at this, perhaps to disguise something that may have otherwise been found."

"You have some notion of what this not-found thing is?" Harshad asked, impressed by her deduction.

"As I have never worked as a wheelwright or a rig smasher, no, I do not." Lucetta tapped her cheek with a slender finger. "You might take the remains to one, however. He may discern what you and I cannot."

Harshad nodded, and discreetly

regarded her face. While very pale like the other women of the village, she had some color on her cheeks. Her hat covered most of her very dark hair, but what he could see gleamed with soft blue glints. Her eyes were the same blue, like polished sapphires. Although her nose was long and thin, it gave her a regal air he thought very comely.

"You should not look at English ladies as you are doing now, Mr. Naveya," Lucetta mentioned as she walked around the heap. "Such looks can be presumed to have more meaning in our society. Also, you are a servant, which requires you should look at your work, or the tips of your shoes."

"Englishwomen do not wish dark men like me to look at them," he guessed.

"Well, I rather like it," she said, and as the sun came out opened her parasol and held it over her head. "My countrymen think me too tall and severe to merit their notice. Your admiration is therefore quite refreshing."

Harshad frowned. "You do not mean that."

"I do, a little." She smiled, and then quickly flattened her lips. "You should know that I am a penniless outcast here, Mr. Naveya. I cannot afford to give offense, particularly to the one gentleman who has bothered to be so mannerly to me. My apologies." She glanced at the clouds billowing up from the horizon. "I think the rain intends to revisit us. I should return home."

"You could join me for tea to wait out the storm, and talk more about English things." He nodded toward the cottage he occupied on the edge of the estate.

"My brother the vicar would never approve of that," Lucetta informed him, and then smiled again. "Happily, I never concern myself with his approval." She offered him her arm.

Once he led her inside his cottage Harshad inspected the front room to assure it was tidy before showing her to the best of his chairs. "If you will sit, Miss Branwen, I will make the tea."

"I would rather help you, if I may?" When he nodded, she followed him into his kitchen. "What is that wonderful smoky smell?"

"Patchouli." As he lit the lamps he

nodded at the urn where he burned the fragrant incense sticks. "It makes the air like home."

"You are from India, of course. I should have guessed that, given the rumors about the colonel." Lucetta began rolling up her sleeves.

Harshad touched her bare forearm. "What have you heard?"

She went still and stared down at his hand, which Harshad just then realized looked almost burnt against the whiteness of her skin. "Only that he came from your country to settle in Renwick after he resigned his commission. Your fingernails are very long, Mr. Naveya."

"I cannot attend to them," he said, dropping his hand. "I am at the house all day, and it is bad luck to do so after the sun sets."

The jewels of her eyes glowed rather than glittered in the lamplight. "You are superstitious."

"I am careful not to walk where there is talk of snakes," Harshad admitted.

A sadness flickered over her face. "I wish I had learned such caution."

Outside the rain began to fall in earnest, and thunder grumbled all around the cottage, but neither of them paid attention to it. Lucetta seemed indifferent to the violence of the weather, and her presence kept Harshad from thinking about it.

Once his water pot boiled, Harshad demonstrated the Hindi method of tea-making by adding Darjeeling leaves, green cardamom and crumbles from a dried cinnamon stick. He allowed the blend to steep for a short time, and then strained it into cups before he added sugar cubes and milk.

"That smells most exotic," Lucetta told him as he presented her with one cup. She did not wrinkle her nose or pretend to taste it but sipped carefully. "Delicious. What is this blend called?"

"Chai." He gestured for her to sit at his small morning table and brought another chair in from the front room to join her. "My mother added peppercorns and dried ginger root to hers, but I do not know where to buy them in England."

"Peppercorns can be had at market, but

for ginger root I think you must visit the apothecary," she advised him.

"I will do that, thank you, Miss." He reached for the plate of sweet cakes he kept on the shelf over his stove and removed the napkin covering them. "My master's cook made these for us so that the memory of home would stay sweet in our mouths. My people call them chomchom."

Lucetta sampled one of the cakes and nodded her approval. "Very sweet and delicate." She tried another bite, chewing it slowly. "They taste of roses."

"They are made with…the water of the flower." Harshad felt frustrated that he did not know the proper term. "It is a very special cake to my people, the Bengali. They even call their beloved ones 'chomchom'."

Her lips curved as she set down the cake. "Have you family back in India, Mr. Naveya?"

"No, Miss." He did not like to think about what had been taken from him, so he rose and began to tidy up. "You have come to visit your brother the vicar?"

"I am presently living with him and his wife, much to our mutual despair." Lucetta's tone seemed indifferent, but Harshad saw the heaviness of emotion causing her shoulders to sag. "It is an unhappy arrangement, but given my lack of funds I must tolerate it."

Harshad could not agree with her. "Family is never tolerable."

She smothered a sound almost like a laugh. "I did not mean to imply that my brother and his wife are unbearable to me. Rather it is the reverse; I am a terrible burden on them."

"No, you are not," he assured her. "You and they are the same blood. If they are penniless, and you are not, would you take them in? Would you call them a burden on you?"

Lucetta's pretty brows drew together. "Of course not, but it is different for–"

"It is the same," he corrected her. "Family is not tolerable. Family is everything. It is love."

"I wish that were true." She stood. "I must return now or they will wonder where I have got to. Thank you for the lovely tea and cakes."

"You are a kind woman, Miss Branwen,

even if you do not wish anyone to know it." Harshad bowed to her. "You should make friends with the young woman who crashed her rig this morning. She is also very kind."

"Mr. Naveya," Lucetta said carefully. "Where, exactly, is this young woman?"

CHAPTER 4

The sound of thunder rattling the windows roused Meredith to open her eyes. After lunching with her the colonel had left her to rest, promising to return to check on her. If he did she could not remember; her slumber had been deep and undisturbed.

As she glanced at the darkened window she saw the flash of lightning, and grimaced. Renwick and the surrounding countryside enjoyed a mild climate, so even an unseasonable storm was generally of short duration. For such a tempest to last for hours would be the talk of the village.

Meredith rose carefully and, feeling no pain from her head, carefully removed the poultice tied to it. Once she plucked the remaining hairpins from their perilous positions she combed her fingers through her messy locks. Without a maid to assist her she would have to resort to the style of her schoolroom days, she decided, and divided her hair into three parts before weaving them into a thick braid, which she pinned over the lump.

My dear girl, he will think you very pretty however your hair is arranged.

Meredith turned her head, but saw no one in the room. For the first time since coming inside the house she felt a tremor of fear. "Who is there? Colonel? Show yourself."

That I fear I cannot do. One of the curtains by the window lifted slowly before wafting back into place. *But I do wish to thank you for admiring The Garden Room. I commissioned it as a tribute to my late wife. Often I came here to sit and think of her in her own gardens. She did so love her flowers.*

The air suddenly seemed very chilly now, making her shiver. "Who are you?"

Emerson Thorne, my dear. I built this place.

"No. You cannot be here." Meredith's heart pounded, and she pressed the heels of her hands against her ears. "No one is speaking to me. It is the lump on my head, nothing more."

I am not here, I suppose, the voice mused. *Nor am I anywhere else, it would seem.*

"I do not believe in ghosts." As she spoke, she saw her breath puff out white with each word. She shut her eyes tightly. "Please, go away."

Even if I wished to, I cannot. The ruins I had removed before they built the house may have been haunted, the unseen man said. *When they invaded the Normans killed all of the poor souls who dwelled here. Perhaps they conspired to keep me here as punishment for desecrating their resting place. I should thank them for that, for there is no place I should rather abide for eternity, Miss Starling.*

Miss Starling.

"Miss Starling."

Meredith opened her eyes to see Colonel Thorne standing over her. When he repeated her name a third time she smiled with relief. "Hello. You are not a ghost."

"Not yet." He pressed his hand over her

forehead. "You are flushed. Do you feel feverish?"

"Not at all." The gentleness of his touch contrasted sharply with his severe expression. "I had the strangest conversation just now."

"Indeed." Thorne pressed the backs of his fingers against her cheek. "Of whom did you dream?"

"Mr. Emerson Thorne, your ancestor. Or rather, his ghost." It seemed utterly fantastic to Meredith that she had spoken with the very first master of Dredthorne Hall. "When you came in, was that curtain over there dancing about in a strange manner? Of course, it wasn't," she said before he could reply. "The windows are closed, and curtains do not dance. You must think me ridiculous."

"I think," Thorne said in a softer tone, "hitting your head has jumbled your thoughts." He glanced around her. "Where is the poultice?"

Meredith lifted her hand to touch her hair. "Not on my head, apparently." Her fingers shook as she reached back and felt the braid pinned there. Had she plaited it in her sleep? It could not be so. "I'm sure someone was here. Perhaps one of your men thought to play a joke."

"They've all spent the last hour having their evening meal together." He drew her hand away from her head. "You had a bad dream, Miss Starling. Nothing more."

"You found me sleeping?" When he nodded Meredith let out a sigh, and then saw the pity in his gaze. "As it happens, I am feeling quite recovered." She sat up and swung her legs over the side of the bed. "Would you permit me downstairs?"

"That is why I am here," he told her. "I thought you might like to join me for dinner." He glanced down at her toes. "Will you allow me to assist you with replacing your slippers?"

"I'd be most grateful." She would keep her composure and stop inviting his pity, Meredith thought, watching Thorne kneel before her and attend to the task. "Will we be enjoying food from India tonight?"

"I do favor their breakfast dishes," Thorne told her. "For dinner, I am more of a traditionalist. Cook has prepared some roasted ham and potatoes." He stood and offered her his hand.

Meredith held it only until she stood, but once she released him he caught her arm and tucked it through his. "I can walk without falling again, Colonel." She hoped.

"Indulge me, Miss Starling," he said. "Too many years have passed since I had the honor of escorting a young lady to dinner."

"Another reason to join Renwick society," she chided as he led her from the room. "Your services as an escort and table companion will be in great demand."

Thorne tucked her arm more securely in his. "You may wish to reserve your judgment on my suitability as such until after the meal."

Once downstairs Thorne guided her across the reception room to where a pair of turbaned footmen stood waiting in front of a faded chinoiserie painting of a gated garden. Beyond the white-painted whorls of iron grew a bewildering variety of flowers and plants, yet as they drew closer Meredith saw no door. The footmen bowed to her and

Thorne before they took hold of concealed handles and open the wall outward, revealing it was not a wall at all but a pair of doors.

"It is called *trompe l'oeil*," Thorne told her. "It means 'to deceive the eye' in French."

"It certainly does." Meredith recovered from her surprise over the doors only to gape again at the interior dining room.

Here Mr. Thorne had taken a turn for the fanciful, outfitting the room panels of dark woods painted with tall, narrow murals, framed by faded inlaid mosaics of shell, brass and moss-colored stone. Although cracks and black streaks left by damp marred all of the portraits, Meredith marveled at their designs. They depicted various temples, settings and figures from ancient mythology such as Herakles, Pandora, and Theseus. Between each panel marble columns stretched from floor to ceiling, their pedestals crowned with tarnished braziers, some still containing the brown, withered remains of plants.

"I have never beheld a room like this," Meredith said, turning around slowly to take in each panel. "I feel as if I have stepped into another time."

"It seems my ancestor had some fondness for the Greeks as well as the French," Thorne said drily. "I fear I possess simpler tastes." He ushered her to the end of the table, where obviously new china and crystal of simple design had been placed. "As you might guess from the settings."

"I share your sentiments, sir." Ever challenged by the alarming delicacy of her mother's heirloom eggshell porcelain and lead crystal, Meredith found the colonel's table arrangements much more attractive and practical. "In time you will leave your stamp on Dredthorne Hall. Mr. Emerson Thorne certainly did. I believe my guest chamber to be a tribute to his late wife, who was very fond of gardening."

Thorne's brows arched. "You know my ancestor exceedingly well."

"One hears old stories about every family in the country," Meredith said, feeling awkward over recounting her own dream as fact.

After the footmen seated them at one

end of the table another servant entered with the first course, a savory soup.

As she ate Meredith wondered how much the colonel would have been obliged to purchase for his household. The local gossips maintained that Emerson Thorne had become fabulously rich, and the heirs that followed him even more so. Of course, no one knew for certain, and it would be beyond the pale to directly inquire. Among the more prosperous gentry those whispers of abundant wealth offended as much as Dredthorne Hall's .

"You are very quiet again, Miss Starling," he said. "Is the food so bad?"

"On the contrary, it is exceptionally delicious." Meredith grimaced. "Forgive me, sir. I'm afraid when I dine with my parents they do most of the talking, and I the listening."

"I did not mean to be critical," he told her. "I am rather glad you are more interested in the food. You look as if you could stand another stone or two."

"You are very kind." Meredith had never minded her narrowness until this very moment. "I have always been thin. The price of too much time in the sickroom, I daresay."

Thorne nodded to the footmen to clear and serve the next course. "You suffered illness as a child?"

"No, my mother insists I was exceedingly healthy as an infant, before my bad luck commenced." She took a sip of water from her glass, and shook her head when the footmen offered her wine. "Keeping to my room to recover from my latest mishap seemed dreadfully dull. I do so love to be out in the sunlight and fresh air."

"As do I," Thorne said. "Although that may be more an occupational habit than actual preference. Do you ride, Miss Starling?"

"My parents forbade my learning." Meredith wondered if he would force her to reveal every inadequacy she possessed. "Doubtless they envisioned me being trampled or thrown off a cliff or something of that nature."

He gave her a measuring look. "Yet they allow you to drive."

"I must, on occasion," she admitted.

"The jolting of the carriage gives my mother the headache, so she rarely goes anywhere. My father is not overly fond of the village, or calling on our neighbors, so he also stays at home. Our manservant sees to the errands, but Mama depends on me to attend to her charitable deliveries."

"It seems you are a doer of good works as well as a spinster in the making." The colonel sat back and made a show of studying her. "I should set you as my example."

The way he looked all over her made Meredith feel oddly heated and breathless, as if all the air in the room had fled. "Only if you wish to be bored and lonely."

Thorne's eyes narrowed. "Perhaps that will soon change. Have you made any plans for your future, Miss Starling?"

She nodded briskly. "Once my father's estate passes to Percival and his future wife, I will inherit a modest income. I hope to acquire a small cottage."

Her yearning for independence didn't seem to please him, for his brows drew together. "You have no other family to invite you to join their household?"

"Mr. Branwen, our vicar, is a distant cousin of my mother's," she admitted. "But I could not impose on him and his wife. I fear he is the last of my relatives."

"I beg to differ." A tall figure entered the dining hall, and regarded them both with her sharp gaze. "Since we are also distant cousins I shall impose on you for introductions, Miss Starling."

Thorne rose along with Meredith and peered at the Indian man hovering a discreet distance behind the new arrival, who showed his master his hands in a helpless gesture.

"Colonel Alistair Thorne, may I introduce to you my cousin, Miss Lucetta Branwen." Meredith felt bewildered by the arrival of the vicar's sister. Once Thorne had bowed she asked, "Forgive me, Miss Branwen, but how is it that you are here?"

"I walked from the village after the first storm, and became caught by the second." She sounded offended, as if the weather had conspired against her. "Colonel, your steward informed me that Miss Starling had also become stranded here. I would offer myself as her chaperon until such time as we may safely depart for home."

"That is very good of you," Meredith said, feeling dismayed again as she turned toward Thorne. Lucetta had presented her proposition almost like a demand. "Would it be a very great imposition, Colonel?"

"Not in the slightest." Thorne gave the older woman a bland smile. "Have you dined, Miss Branwen?"

"Mr. Naveya was kind enough to provide me with tea, but I would be grateful for some dinner." She glanced up and frowned. "Are you aware that you have a great many cobwebs infesting this room?"

To Meredith's relief Lucetta proved more amicable than critical, and spent the remainder of the meal discussing the various merits of country life. Thorne seemed unsurprised to learn the vicar's sister had worked most of her life as a governess in London. When Meredith inquired as to her last position, however, Lucetta offered only a vague answer and quickly changed the subject to inquire about the accident.

"Why would you take this road if you

meant to visit the village?" the older woman asked once Meredith had described the events that had brought her to Dredthorne Hall. "You do know that it leads away from Renwick."

"I do." How would she explain herself? Feeling some hair against her cheek, Meredith brushed back the strands. "I meant only to take a short ride before I attended to Mama's errands."

"That seems a pleasant way to enjoy the fresh air," Thorne put in. "Doubtless just as you sought with your walk, Miss Branwen."

Now Lucetta appeared as unsettled as Meredith felt. "Of course."

WHEN THEY FINISHED THEIR MEAL, both ladies refused dessert, and then offered to retreat to the sitting room so that Thorne could indulge in the customary habit of an after-dinner port and cigar. As he stood to escort them Thorne noticed Meredith again brushing at her face. From the movement of the hair strands something seemed to be tugging them free of her braid.

"Colonel, may I examine the Pandora panel there?" Meredith asked, gesturing toward the back of the room.

"If you wish, of course." He watched her approach the wall with her hand slightly raised. "Is there something the matter?"

"I thought I felt a draft coming from this spot, but perhaps I imagined it." As she drew closer she peered at the box in the figure's hands. "There appears to be a crack in the paint." She reached out to touch the portrait.

"Such things are common in old paintings, Cousin," Lucetta said, frowning, and then went still as something clicked and the painting seemed to swing out. "Egad. That is surely not."

Meredith glanced over her shoulder, surprised by how alarmed her cousin looked. "Sir, this is a door, not a wall."

Thorne joined her, and took hold of the edge of the hinged panel to open it wider. Behind the painting lay a large dark space that smelled of dust and old paper. "It seems you have discovered another room, Miss Starling."

"Now I feel a proper adventurer," Meredith told him. "What could be hidden away behind the walls of a dining room?"

"Perhaps the servants once used it for dish storage." Lucetta brought the candelabra from the table and offered it to him. "Here, this should provide some illumination."

Thorne watched the flames flicker. "Your cousin did not imagine that draft, Miss Branwen." He stepped inside, and then turned to survey the glassy upper walls of the small chamber.

Mirrors stretched from floor to ceiling, interrupted only by cases containing hundreds of books. Between two of the cases sat a small, cold fireplace with several odd instruments on the mantle.

"The servants must have been very well-read," the vicar's sister said as she peered inside.

Meredith's eyes rounded. "A secret library, how marvelous."

Her cousin did not appear as impressed. "Whoever built this likely wished to hide these books for some nefarious reason. There may be creatures infesting them as well. Cousin, we should leave this to the colonel to examine."

"Oh, must we?" Meredith turned to Thorne. "Of course, if you wish some privacy we will leave, but I've never before seen a hidden room."

"Perhaps more light will provide some reassurance for your cousin." He handed her the candles, and went to fetch two lamps from the dining table. He handed one to Lucetta before entering the concealed room and placing the other on the small desk at the back of the chamber. The mirrored walls reflected the lights until the room took on a soft glow.

"It is incredible," Meredith murmured.

Lucetta sniffed. "Such displays of vanity generally are."

Thorne found curtains behind the desk, and when he drew them back he saw an inward-curved window that had been painted black. Air seeped in through a large crack in the lower pane, and when he peered through it he saw the hall's rain-washed front steps. "Here is the source of your draft, Miss Starling."

She nodded, but then her attention strayed to the tarnished apparatus lining the mantle above the hearth. "These instruments here appear to be scientific in nature. Was Mr. Emerson Thorne engaged in some sort of research, I wonder?"

"No one seems to know what the man did while he lived here," Thorne told her. "The estate agent called him a staunch recluse."

"Some of these devices are used to make measurements of stars," Lucetta said as she inspected the collection. "I have seen their like at the British Museum. Perhaps he had a keen interest in astronomy. Then again, gentlemen often purchase such scientific trifles simply to appear as if they do."

"The mirrors make the room seem to go on forever," Meredith murmured as she turned around, and smiled as she saw her reflection repeated over and over in the glass panels. "I have heard looking glasses being faced to produce such an effect in ball rooms."

"Strange that they have never blackened

over the years. Given the draft, it is remarkable that they or any of these books survived." Lucetta ran her finger along the surface of the desk and then inspected the tip. "This should be blanketed in a layer of dust, but it is spotless. The crack in the window must be very recent, Colonel."

"I agree. When there is no air to enter the chamber everything within is preserved, as it is in a tomb." Thorne picked up a crystal ink well, removing the silver lid before showing the contents to Meredith. "Still liquid. My ancestor must have retreated here to write his letters, and read his favorite books."

"May I, Colonel?" When he nodded Lucetta went to a shelf and took down a slim volume. "This was printed a century past, and yet the pages are as crisp and unmarked as if they came from the press yesterday."

"You ladies may borrow anything you wish to read," he told her.

The older woman nodded, and made a methodical inspection of the contents of the bookcases. Meredith drifted from one shelf to another, smiling as she recognized certain titles and frowning over others.

Thorne joined her at the children's section and glanced over her shoulder to see the storybook she had opened. "Do you favor fairytales, Miss Starling?"

"I did, once." She showed him a page depicting fairy-like creatures frolicking in a flowery meadow. "My favorite was the story of the Swan Princes, although it always made me cry in the end."

"I am not familiar with that tale," Thorne admitted.

"The princess in the story labors very hard to free her many brothers from a curse which transformed them into swans. A handsome King falls in love with her, and carries her off to marry her, but even that does not dissuade her. She even risks her life to save her family. Yet despite her labors and her sacrifice, in the end she is unable to entirely save the youngest. He must go on through life with one arm and a swan's wing." She gave him a rueful smile. "I thought it so terribly unfair, but I suppose most things seem so, when we are children."

He thought of his own affliction. "Such resentments end with maturity."

"I daresay they should," Meredith said, looking a little embarrassed now.

"Colonel Thorne," Lucetta said from behind them. "Might I consult with you on the merits of these French novels in the dining room, where the light is better?"

Thorne suspected the vicar's sister hadn't the slightest interest in any novels, but nonetheless accompanied her out of the hidden room. "My French is not what it should be, but you may find the novels of Dumas entertaining."

"The French seldom amuse anyone but themselves," she admitted. "What I truly wish to discuss is my cousin's presence here, Colonel, and the threat that poses. I must ask you to do something to help protect her reputation."

He nodded. "I am at your service, Miss Branwen."

"Thank you, sir." Her tone softened a degree. "I intend to say that I have been here at Dredthorne since my cousin's accident occurred. I will claim to have witnessed it, and never to have left her side for a moment. Will you support me in these falsehoods, that together we may shield Meredith?"

"Of course." Thorne suddenly liked the vicar's sister much more than he had expected to. "You are very kind."

"As her cousin I can do no less." She fussed with the cuffs of her sleeves before she glanced over at the entry to the hidden room. "My brother has often mentioned Meredith in his letters. She has suffered enough misfortune for three lifetimes." In a quieter voice she said, "Your steward and I found the remains of her rig smashed all over the road. It looked quite deliberate; perhaps an effort to conceal the true cause of the accident."

"Someone tampered with that rig before she set out," he said, keeping his voice as low as hers. "I am convinced."

"We should discuss this further before she is returned to her parents, if possible." She looked up as Meredith emerged from the library, and then down at the title page of the book in her hands. "Voltaire, how interesting. A decidedly polemic radical, but then propriety rarely troubles the

French. Have you chosen a book to read, Cousin?"

"No, I have found something else," Meredith said, her eyes dancing with excitement. "I uncovered another hidden space, behind the shelves of the children's books."

Thorne and Lucetta followed her back to the spot, from which she had removed all of the books from the case. This revealed a panel of stained glass fashioned to resemble an open window.

Thorne bent over, and through the glass saw what Meredith had: a closet-size space filled entirely with more shelves of books.

"You've found a cache." He straightened and looked at the empty case in front of it. "I cannot see how to get at it."

"Allow me." Lucetta stepped closer to run her fingers carefully along the sides of the case. She hesitated, and then pressed firmly on one spot, and an audible click sounded before the case began to swing out.

"How did you know to do that?" Meredith asked.

"I have seen work like this before in a

few other country houses," Lucetta said as she straightened. "I believe this may have been modeled after the work of Nicholas Owen."

"Papa told me about him," Meredith said. "He lived during the reign of Elizabeth the first, at least, until he was put to death."

"He was a Jesuit as well as a carpenter, and something of a genius at creating secret passages and spaces." Her cousin wrapped her arms around her waist as she studied the concealing shelves again. "Your ancestor must have wished that the right sort of person should find this particular cache. A feminine person, I should think."

"Why make such an assumption?" Thorne asked. "Anyone might have found it."

The older woman gave him a slightly sour smile. "How many grown men do you know favor reading children's books?"

He uttered a short laugh. "I see your point."

"Governesses are generally not permitted to freely remove books from a library. They make any such requests of the lady of the house, that she might first approve their selection for the children." Lucetta turned to Meredith. "Indeed, Cousin, I believe that he wished someone like you to find this."

"I am not the lady of this house." Meredith felt mortified that she had blurted that out, and quickly added, "What would be the purpose?"

"I cannot tell you." Her cousin's expression grew shuttered. "All men hide their secrets."

Thorne picked up a candle and held it closer to the opened panel. "It seems to be another collection of books." He reached in through the small space and retrieved one volume, which he handed to Lucetta. She drew back and carried it closer to one of the lamps.

"These are not books, Colonel," the older woman said. She showed him the pages inside, which were covered in elegant script. "They are journals."

"Surely not?" Meredith sounded incredulous, and bent down to peer into the hidden panel before she looked up at Thorne. "They all do seem to have the same binding."

"Can you make out the first entry in that one, Miss Branwen?" Thorne asked.

"It says here: 'August seventh, morning,'" Lucetta said, reading from the first page. "'Construction continues today on the west wing. I escape it as often as I may, for the noise made by the masons is prodigious, and my tolerance decidedly not.'" She glanced up at Thorne. "It may have been written by Mr. Emerson Thorne himself, as the place was being built."

"There are more than a hundred in there, I should think," Meredith said. "How could one gentleman write so many?"

"He spent his final years as a widower, and a recluse," Thorne reminded her. "Doubtless he intended them as a memoir."

"He would not wish his most private thoughts to fall into just any hands, so he then concealed them." Meredith caught her breath. "Colonel, these journals could contain all the secrets of Dredthorne Hall."

"You are being overly romantic, Cousin," Lucetta said sharply. "These may be nothing more than estate ledgers."

At that moment a tendril of wind came through the window, and caught the pages of the open journal, turning them in a flurry.

Thorne felt the oddest sense of no longer being alone with the two women. "Perhaps we should delve into that subject tomorrow."

* * *

BEFORE THEY LEFT the hidden library Meredith carefully replaced the books on the shelves concealing the stained-glass window.

"There." She stood back to inspect her handiwork. "It is covered again, so only the three of us know it is there."

"I will take its secrets to the grave," Lucetta promised, her tone slightly mocking. "Colonel, I believe I will retire for the evening, if that is acceptable. I think Meredith should do the same."

"Of course. Follow me." Thorne set down the journal she had handed him and led them out of the room.

Meredith was glad to see that her cousin would have the bedchamber across from hers, and peeked inside to see a lovely old canopied bed draped in white lace. "It is a very handsome room."

"Would you join me for a few minutes, cousin?" When she nodded, Meredith turned to Thorne. "Thank you for an interesting evening, Colonel."

"My pleasure, Miss Branwen. Miss Starling." Thorne gave Meredith a lingering look before he bowed and withdrew.

Sitting down beside the crackling fire in the bedchamber made Meredith sigh with pleasure. "I have never had such a good time as this. Can you believe we are the first ladies to visit Dredthorne Hall in fifty years? The house is a veritable treasure chest of wonders."

Lightning flared outside, followed by an ominous boom of thunder that made the old glass panes rattle. Yet even that sound made the room feel even cozier. No matter how terrible the weather grew, the house protected them.

Why does no one else see what I do in Dredthorne Hall? Meredith realized she had said that out loud, and grimaced at her cousin. "I don't understand why the villagers so dislike this house. I think it the loveliest of places."

"No one can mistake your enthusiasm, my dear." Lucetta sat down across for her and regarded her steadily. "You do know, however, that you should not have remained here alone with the colonel."

"Yes, of course." Meredith glanced at the window. "I would have walked home, Cousin, but for the storm. The colonel would not permit me leave."

"I assumed as much. I only wish you had been driving by the parsonage, and then we might have avoided this entire situation." She sighed. "Nevertheless, I believe with some slight alteration of the facts we can preserve your reputation. I will return with you to your home tomorrow. You will then tell your parents that we met on the road, and I came with you to Dredthorne to wait out the storm."

"That is not the truth," Meredith protested. "Nor should I wish to lie to my parents."

"Do you *wish* to be ruined forever, or have the colonel forced to make an offer of marriage?" Lucetta demanded, her expression stern now. "If word of your escapade gets out, one of those two things will be the result."

"My parents will tell no one," Meredith insisted. "They know I would never behave improperly. Once I have explained about my injury and the colonel's carriage being repaired, they will understand I could do nothing else."

"What of your mother's friends, when she lets the truth slip to them? Or your father, when he comes here to demand that Thorne make an honest woman of you, as any man should?" Lucetta raised her brows. "What can be done about that? Would you repay Thorne's kindness with the ruination of his character, or the loss of his freedom to choose a wife?"

"There is no reason for those things to be done." Meredith wrapped her good arm over her sling. "I did nothing improper, Cousin. I was hurt, and the colonel helped me. That is the truth."

"No one will care what actually occurred between you, my dear." The older woman's expression turned bitter. "Why do you think they call it keeping up appearances? Because everything is about how it appears. You have spent many hours alone in the company of a man you do not know. That is enough to ruin your name forever."

"Very well." Meredith stood up, unable to bear another moment of Lucetta's harping on propriety. "I will not lie to my parents, but I will not dispute anything you say to them. Goodnight, Cousin."

When she returned to her room Meredith was careful to first toe off her slippers before she walked across the slippery rug. One of the colonel's servants had lit the lamps and turned down the bed linens; all she had to do was remove her dress, and...

Meredith glanced down at her sling, and then tried to reach the buttons on the back of her gown with her good arm. She could not manage to free even one of them.

"Drat." If only she dared utter some oaths. "Perhaps I will simply rip it off, and prance about in my underclothes."

She sat down on the window seat and leaned her brow against the cold glass. Long ago she had learned to quell her temper, for to become angry over things she could not change served no purpose. Of course, she would not destroy the only dress she had to wear; she would return to her cousin's room to ask for her assistance. Or she might forego comfort and sleep in her gown, for she did not wish to speak to Lucetta again until her temper subsided.

How could she think that Papa would force the Colonel to offer for me?

Neither of Meredith's parents ever spoke to her about the possibility of marriage. When she was younger her father had made it clear that she would not be presented at court or enjoy a season in the city. Both were too costly, and Lady Starling felt convinced that allowing her daughter to go to London would end in disaster or death. None of the eligible young men in the area had ever taken an interest in her; Meredith had trouble finding one willing even to dance with her at assemblies. Doubtless her parents assumed, as she did, that she would end a spinster.

While Meredith had always known she would never marry, she felt some curiosity about the intimate relationship between a husband and wife. She had tried twice to ask her mother about what happened after marriage. Both times Lady Starling had suffered an immediate onset of the headache that resulted in her retiring to her bedchamber.

The novels Meredith sometimes filched from her father's book room had provided only vague clues that involved the man coming to his wife's room and sharing kisses and much embracing. After reading Desdemona's shocking death scene in Shakespeare's Othello, however, Meredith had resolved never to allow any man to enter her bedchamber in the night.

Should he come to her, Meredith thought Colonel Thorne would not attempt to strangle her. He would touch her with those clever hands of his, and gaze at her with his crystalline eyes, and then perhaps touch his lips to hers...and then she would surely swoon.

Disturbed by her own desires, Meredith went to the bed, and lay down on her side to avoid the discomfort of her gown's buttons against her spine. Exhaustion suddenly swamped her, and she closed her eyes. She would rest for a moment, and then seek Lucetta's assistance with her dress. Only for a moment…

An unsteady, heavy sound roused Meredith from a sound sleep. For a moment she thought she'd dreamt it, and then it came again. Gingerly she pushed herself up to look at the door. Had someone knocked? Was it morning? No, the window remained dark. "Hello?"

A muffled groan answered her.

Carefully she climbed off the bed and made her way to the door. When she opened it, she saw that no one stood outside. She leaned out to peruse the hall, but only shadows filled it. Then she heard the groaning again, more distant now, as if it came from the opposite side of the house. A particular loud thump made her flinch, and then everything fell silent.

"What are you doing?"

Meredith uttered a small cry as Lucetta came out of the darkness, her tall form wrapped in a pale coverlet. "Heavens, Cousin, you scared the wits out of me."

"I am sorry for that." The older woman's

dark hair hung in a long, thick braid that twitched as she glanced both ways down the hall. "Sounds from the wind tormenting a loose shutter woke me from my sleep."

Was that what had caused the eerie noise? Meredith had thought the sound more like a voice of someone in torment. But she was being fanciful; she'd been half-asleep when she'd heard it.

"The same happened to me." Meredith grimaced down at the wrinkled condition of her gown. "I must have fallen asleep before I could ask for your assistance with my buttons."

"Come, then, and I will attend to them." Lucetta urged her back into the room, closing the door firmly before she regarded the chair by the fireplace. "Perhaps I should sleep in here tonight."

"I'm not a child for you to safeguard," Meredith said, and immediately regretted the harsh protest when she saw pain in her cousin's bleak expression. "Forgive me, I don't mean to snap."

"Why shouldn't you? I've been treating you like a child all evening." Her cousin went around her and began releasing her buttons. "It's simply that…one should not wander in a strange house, particularly in the night. You may stumble across secrets that you never wished to find."

Meredith suspected that Lucetta wasn't referring to Dredthorne Hall now. The unsteadiness in her voice made all her own ire vanish. Once she had finished with the buttons she turned to face her. "If you truly want to stay, then of course you must. I will take the chair, and you the bed."

"Nonsense. As you well reminded me, you are not a child." The older woman helped her out of her gown and then forced a smile. "I will be just across the hall if you have need of me. Good-night, my dear."

Something dreadful had happened to her cousin in London, Meredith suspected, to make her so fearful. But what could do that to a strong, purposeful woman like Lucetta?

CHAPTER 5

Breakfast at Dredthorne, Meredith discovered, proved as pleasing as dinner, with one unexpected, added delight—Colonel Thorne had it served on the garden terrace. While the flower beds had been cleared in preparation for the winter, fall leaves still adorned most of the trees. A few birds flitted about the branches as they chirped and sang. The sun embellished the ground with pale golden light, adding a subtle glow to the house's weathered outer walls.

"What a marvelous notion to breakfast out here," Meredith told the colonel and her cousin as she joined them. "How lovely it smells out here from the rain."

"I thought you might approve." Thorne, whose dark riding coat, buff leather breeches and dusty boots implied he had begun his morning on horseback, sat down across from her. "I have sent my stablemaster to hire suitable transport for you both. Miss Branwen, would you be so kind as to reassure Miss Starling's parents as to her safe accommodations here at Dredthorne?"

"That was my plan, Colonel." Lucetta gave Meredith a sideways glance. "I will explain everything, of course."

"As you wish, Cousin." She had agreed to do so last night, so she would have to keep her word, but she still disliked the entire scheme. To keep from showing her resentment she turned to inspect a platter of rice and fish being offered by the footman.

"I am curious, Colonel." The older woman took a sip of her spiced tea before she nodded at the house. "What do you plan to do with the library Meredith found in your dining room?"

He frowned. "I have little time for

reading. Once my steward sees to repairing the window, I will summon a bookseller to make an offer for the lot."

"Not before you catalog the contents, surely," Meredith protested. As his brows rose she quickly added, "Some of the editions could be very valuable, and do you not wish to first examine Mr. Emerson Thorne's journals?"

"At present the house demands all my attention." The colonel's gaze shifted above her head, and his mouth thinned. "Over time a roof leak has caused flooring to rot in the servants' quarters and in other rooms below them. I must assess the extent of the damage, and procure workmen to see to the repairs. The number of livable cottages remains inadequate, and my men cannot spend the winter sleeping in the stables."

"Certainly not." Lucetta looked as if she approved. "If you need recommendations for the workmen, my brother knows every man of worth in his parish. He would be happy to assist."

They were talking as if the matter were decided, Meredith thought. "I catalogued our family library for my father last spring, Colonel. It does take time, but to know what you possess makes the effort worthwhile. I found several valuable first editions that belonged to my great-grandfather that Papa had never seen."

Thorne's stern expression softened. "If you truly wish to see it done, Miss Starling, perhaps you should undertake the work. You do have the necessary experience and knowledge, and you discovered the library. If you are agreeable, the task is yours."

The prospect of returning to Dredthorne and spending more time within its walls made only one answer possible for Meredith. "I would be delighted, Colonel."

"Then we must come to an amicable arrangement." As Lucetta stiffened the colonel turned his bright blue gaze on her. "Miss Branwen, if you are not otherwise engaged, would you be willing to extend your services as chaperone to your cousin?"

The older woman looked as if she intended to refuse. At that moment the colonel's steward came to the table with a bowl of sliced berries. He met Lucetta's gaze and gave her a slight bow before retreating.

Why, they like each other, Meredith thought, recalling that the steward had served her cousin tea and cakes.

Lucetta inclined her head toward Harshad before she regarded Thorne. "Perhaps we might first discuss this in more practical detail before I answer. If we are to do this work, how often would you wish us to come to the house, and where would it be done? Surely not in that tiny hidden room."

As they spoke about the arrangements Meredith could barely contain her excitement. Spending a night at Dredthorne had been a blessing, not a curse. For once her bad luck had resulted in granting her dearest wish. She would be returning to Dredthorne to explore the mystery of the hidden library, where doubtless she would uncover new wonders.

"Very well," Lucetta said at last. "If we are not otherwise engaged, Meredith, then we may come any time during the day that we wish. I suggest we work from midmorning until four. The colonel will provide luncheon, and obtain a rig for my use so I may collect you and take you home."

They didn't trust her to drive herself, she realized, her high spirits deflating a little. Having Lucetta at the reins would provide reassurance for her mother, however, who might otherwise forbid Meredith's return. "That sounds sensible."

They finished the meal in a companionable silence, at which point the stable master arrived with the hired carriage. Thorne walked out with them to the drive, where he helped Lucetta up before taking Meredith's hand in his.

The bright sun made his eyes glitter like snow on a clear lake, but the smile he gave her seemed warmly genuine. "Until we meet again, Miss Starling, tread carefully in those slippers."

"I will, Colonel Thorne. Thank you for everything." Her heart skipped a beat as he bowed over her hand, and for a moment she thought he might kiss her knuckles. But no, he only straightened and helped her into the carriage.

As the driver started away, Meredith turned to look back. For once the house didn't captivate her attention; for Thorne himself effortlessly held her gaze. He seemed as confident and aloof as before, but the strangest sense of having abandoned him came over her.

Soon I will return. This is where I belong.

The notion seemed terribly presumptuous, but Meredith could not remember the last time she had felt as safe as she did at Dredthorne Hall. Every day in her life had begun with her trapped between hope and despair. Would she go unscathed, or be struck down again by her bad luck? Sometimes it had taken all of her nerve simply to leave her bedchamber.

When she had tripped and fallen down the stairs last month, Meredith remembered her last thought before blacking out was wishing her neck would break, and that would be the last of all her terrible misfortunes. Now that she had come inside this amazing house, she realized how foolish her dark thoughts had been.

There is so much more to know in this world.

With this endeavor Meredith would also have more time to spend with her cousin, whom she suspected needed a confidante. Lucetta might present herself as rigid and stern, but beneath that façade lay a kind, generous soul. Something had happened to her, some heavy burden that she carried alone. Meredith felt sure she could be of help to her cousin, and possibly free her of the shadows from the past that still haunted her.

The same was true of Thorne, isolating himself from others because he had been too long away from England. He had endured much while serving king and country, Meredith guessed, and wished to put it all behind him. She could help him adjust to his new situation in life and, with Percival's help, introduce him to their neighbors and friends. While she might be doomed to ending a spinster, Meredith hoped someday soon to see him married.

In fact, she would do everything in her power to help him find a good and loving wife.

* * *

ALTHOUGH MEREDITH SEEMED unaware that she was forming an attachment to Alistair Thorne, Lucetta decided to keep silent on the matter. She had no right to interfere, nor did she wish to shatter her young cousin's dreams.

She knew that Meredith had yet to understand that the heart played almost no role in securing an appropriate match. While he might indulge her cousin's adoration for his decrepit house, Thorne would soon have to find a wife suited to his situation in life. His wealth and good looks would draw the attention of every unattached heiress in the shire. Although regarded as reputable, the Starlings had only modest connections. Their limited income came from their estate, which had been long ago entailed. Likely Meredith's pretty face and sweet disposition would be her only dowry.

Romantic disappointment loomed ahead for her young cousin; hastening its arrival would be cruel.

Lucetta felt rather cross with herself for

agreeing to serve as a chaperone, as Thorne had obviously maneuvered her into that. Still, it would give her something to do. She couldn't bear to be cooped up with Jeffrey's timorous wife every day. Her brother would also be relieved to have her gone; she'd distracted him from his duties long enough. As for Harshad Naveya, whom she liked very much, she suspected they would become good friends as they looked after Thorne and Meredith.

Once they arrived at Starling House, Lucetta felt startled by how visibly the manor showed its age. Meredith's parents had created a mirage of respectability by lime-washing the exterior, but cracks show plainly through the opaque coating. Gaps in the roofing from missing shingles showed the black of mildew, hinting at the likelihood of leaks within. Of the six chimneys she could see, only one produced smoke.

The small surrounding property also displayed signs of ongoing neglect. The trees badly needed pruning, and the gardens on either side of the manor had not yet been prepared for winter. Two urns of withered rose canes flanking the front entry to the manor added a distinct epitaphic air.

With the Starlings' estate in such decline, Lucetta knew they had no money to tempt a suitor for Meredith.

A maid servant came to help them down from the carriage, and bobbed before she said, "Miss, I beg you come to the morning room at once. Milord is with milady there, and Mr. Percival and his mother have come." Her voice fell to a hushed whisper. "They're all ever so upset, Miss."

"Thank you, Annie." Meredith sighed before she said to Lucetta, "The whole family has assembled, but at least they have not sent for the militia." She glanced at the manor before she added, "Mama will likely be very vexed with me. She becomes a bit loud in such circumstances."

"You have been gone an entire day without her knowing what happened," she reminded her as they went inside. "She is entitled to considerable vexation."

Even forewarned, Lucetta felt startled by Lady Starling's reaction to seeing her daughter enter the room.

"Meredith, you are *alive*." The distraught woman uttered the words like a wail, and then fell back on her divan, gasping and fluttering her hands over her face and bosom. "I thought you dead or drowned or trampled by horses. Yesterday, when you did not return, I told your father you had come to harm. Last night I could not sleep and feared I should die of a broken heart."

Abruptly Lady Starling fainted, and chaos ensued.

The maid servant ran for smelling salts. Lord Starling leaned over his wife, alternately trying to revive her and glaring at his daughter. Meredith hurried to kneel down beside the divan, only to be swatted away by her father. A tall man in military uniform, presumably Meredith's cousin, came closer, peered, and then retreated. He put his arm around an elderly woman who kept calling Lady Starling "Sister" as she implored her not to die.

Meredith stepped back, her expression that of someone seeing a tiresome scene being repeated.

"I am sorry, Cousin." She gave Lucetta an embarrassed look. "Mama hasn't swooned since I became locked in the pantry for the night when I was twelve. Perhaps we should leave them to calm down."

"Stay there and permit me to manage this." Lucetta cleared her throat so loudly everyone in the room stared at her, even Lady Starling. "My lord, my lady, as you see your daughter is quite alive. I am happy to report that, aside from a slight injury to her arm, she is also well. Perhaps you will allow me to explain what has happened to keep her from home."

Meredith's mother peered at her. "I know you. Only I cannot think now, so your name escapes me." She dropped back against the divan. "Oh, Husband, I am so addled."

"As you've every right to be, my dear," Lord Starling told her in a soothing tone before scowling at Lucetta. "Who is this woman, Meredith?"

"Forgive me," Meredith said, and made hasty introductions before she said to Percival, "Miss Branwen is the vicar's sister, recently returned from London. The Branwens are also our cousins."

"I did not realize you were family, ma'am." Percival clicked his heels together, standing very straight before he bowed.

"We are but very distantly related, Lieutenant." Lucetta eyed the glittering number of medals adorning the younger man's jacket, which indicated that he had distinguished himself often during his service. "You are on leave from your regiment?"

"No, ma'am. After my father died I resigned my commission to come home and look after my dear mother." Percival smiled at the elderly woman. "We came as soon as we heard Cousin Meredith had gone missing. Mama and I count ourselves fortunate to live so close to Starling House, for it allows us to visit the family whenever they are willing to tolerate our company."

"Oh, never say that, Percival," Lady Starling, now evidently recovered, scolded him. "If not for you, Meredith would surely be dead and buried now."

Lucetta heard Percival's mother sniff rather loudly.

"You are too generous, as always, Aunt." Percival beamed with delight. "So, how do you find it here, Miss Branwen? Do you mean to make our village your permanent home, or are you longing for the excitement of London again?"

"I have not yet decided." Lucetta disliked the way the Starlings fawned over their nephew while showing no actual concern for their daughter. "Perhaps we may speak on the matter after I have related what occurred on the road to Renwick yesterday."

Offering an abbreviated version of Meredith's rig accident, and describing the storm's violence, Lucetta assured the couple that there had been no choice for them but to impose on Alistair Thorne's hospitality. At this point Lady Starling sat up, her expression newly aghast, while her husband muttered under his breath and Lavinia covered her mouth with trembling fingers. Only Percival seemed relieved to hear that Meredith had been provided with care and shelter by their new neighbor.

"Be assured, my lady, that Colonel Thorne acted the perfect gentleman while we stayed at the hall," Lucetta said at last. "I also remained at Meredith's side the entire time."

"You spent the night in that wretched place," Lavinia whispered, her tone strangled. "Surely the two of you have been cursed."

Percival patted her shoulder. "Never fear, Mama. The colonel cannot marry them both. That would be against the law."

Lucetta wondered if while shining his medals the lieutenant had inhaled too many vapors from the polish.

"I should never let *my* child near that wicked man," his mother mumbled.

"Do you think to blame me for this, Sister?" Lady Starling demanded. "I have told my daughter time and again to stay away from that dreadful place. All the talk of it and that curse is most unseemly. Thorne is nothing to us."

Meredith's shoulders slumped. "Mama, the colonel was very kind to me. I would call him our friend."

"Would you now?" Her mother's contempt faded as she glanced at her husband, and something wordless passed between them. She then smiled at her daughter. "That is good of you, my dear. We must show the appropriate gratitude toward Thorne. Perhaps that will demonstrate to the village how to behave in a civilized manner."

"I daresay it shall do much to dispel these ridiculous rumors," Lord Starling said, nodding.

Lucetta felt confused by the abrupt approval. After the uproar she had felt certain the Starlings would not want Meredith to go near Dredthorne again. She had been trying to think of how to broach the subject to assure their consent to their scheme, or was she more concerned with escaping her own unhappy situation at the parsonage?

She thought of the signs of neglect she had seen outside the manor, and then realized what was happening. The Starlings knew Thorne had inherited a sizable fortune. They had a daughter they could not endower whom he had rescued. Advantageous marriages had been arranged on far less obligations. Doubtless they now saw him as an answer to their prayers.

In any case, it seemed the right moment

for Lucetta to mention their plan, as long as she presented it in an acceptable manner.

"Since Meredith and I share a love of books, Lady Starling, I thought she might help me with cataloging one of Colonel Thorne's libraries," Lucetta said. "If you can spare her, may I call for her tomorrow morning? I will do all the driving."

"Yes, of course. When you see him again, do give the colonel our deepest thanks for helping our girl in her distress." Meredith's mother made a weak gesture. "All of you, please go now. I must rest now that she is home."

Percival and his mother walked out with Lucetta, and he handed her up into the carriage before sketching another elegant bow. "A pleasure to make your acquaintance, Miss Branwen."

"Good afternoon, Lieutenant. Mrs. Starling." She watched him escort his mother to an older rig a short distance away. Their horse appeared to be more suited to plowing than driving, and started off at a crawling pace. It seemed none of the family had deep pockets.

Meredith told the driver to wait before

she leaned in to say, "You saved me, Cousin."

Lucetta could see the happiness gleaming in her eyes, and felt mollified to know she had been responsible. "Be ready to leave at eleven, my dear."

Within a week Meredith's parents had mostly forgiven her for the rig accident that had stranded her at Dredthorne Hall, at least by their avoidance of the subject and her. Lord Starling said very little to her during the one meal they shared, and remained in his study with the door closed for the rest of the day. While at home Meredith made sure to stay out of her mother's path, although Lady Starling made that easy by keeping to her bed chamber. Aware that their mistress's distress made her sensitive to any noise, the servants tiptoed through their duties, sometimes casting resentful looks at Meredith.

What Meredith lived for were the happy

hours she spent with Lucetta at Dredthorne Hall. From the first day Colonel Thorne had made them welcome and comfortable, setting up the large reception room at the back of the house. The wide oval room, with white walls now faded to a slightly yellowed cream color, had been sumptuously decorated with heavily gilded carvings and molding. Although tarnished and speckled by age, the prisms of the twin grand chandeliers still reflected sunlight in rainbow-banded patches all around them.

"It is like working inside a tiara," Lucetta claimed when Meredith pointed out the charming effect. "But at least we will not be required to waltz. I am a dreadful dancer."

Thorne provided them with desks, tables, chairs, ledgers and writing supplies for their use. Footmen brought carts loaded with books from the hidden library. Two fireplaces kept them warm, and the large windows provided excellent natural light. They had agreed to start with the printed books, which they would catalog while the colonel looked through the hand-written journals in private. Meredith understood he would first wish to read them himself, but hoped he would allow her and Lucetta to examine at least some of them. The old books she enjoyed, but the chance to read what Emerson Thorne had written would thrill her to no end.

Mr. Naveya kept them supplied with tea, cakes and sandwiches in the morning, and served luncheon in the dining room before they left for the day. At times the colonel would leave his labors upstairs to join them for the meal, during which Meredith and Lucetta would report on their progress.

"Dividing the books by language first will help reunite missing volumes, Alistair," Meredith told him after she described their organizational method. She still felt a little shy using his given name, but Thorne had insisted the three of them forsake formality while alone. "We found several of the French and German books were shelved in a confusing jumble."

"One of the cases may have fallen over in the past, causing the displacement," Lucetta put in. "Most of the books found out of order show slight damage to the covers and spines." She nodded toward the

Pandora panel. "I would like to have another look at the shelving now, and see the number of books yet to be removed. We may need more tables in our work room to compile the different collections."

"Take Harshad with you," Thorne said, his voice rasping slightly as he finished his tea. "I would not like to find you buried beneath another collapse, Lucetta."

The older woman went into the library with the steward, leaving the two of them alone.

"Have you made much progress with the repairs to the upstairs flooring, sir?" Meredith asked as the footmen began to clear the table. "We have heard the sounds of the men you hired working."

"At present they must clear out the rotted wood, which is more extensive than I reckoned. It will be some weeks before the replacement floors can be installed." He rose to his feet, and then hesitated. "While your cousin is occupied, would you care to see one of the staircase towers? Lucetta mentioned your interest in them."

She only just managed not to hop up and down with delight. "Yes, please."

To access the tower Thorne had to lead her through the kitchen, where his cook and two other men were busy already preparing food for the evening meals. They did not stop working but simply nodded as Meredith and Thorne passed. She smiled at them as she breathed in the piquant scent of curry and spices.

At the arched door to the tower Thorne stopped and gestured for her to step to one side. Then he pressed his hand on one side of the panel, which swung out with a faintly whining creak.

"A hidden spring latch?" Meredith asked.

He nodded. "My ancestor had some curious notions about doors," he told her as he guided her over the threshold. "The other tower entry is fitted in the same fashion."

Once inside Meredith looked up and gasped. The spiraling staircase seemed to extend up forever, although she knew it had to stop at the attic level. She then shifted slightly, and saw that the very top of the tower roof had been painted with a spiral that grew smaller and smaller until it disappeared into its own center.

"Have you climbed to the top yet?" she asked, feeling breathless.

"At present the water damage makes that too dangerous. Every landing has been rotted above the first floor." Thorne came to stand beside her. "I have been invited to an assembly at Lady Hardiwick's tomorrow evening. She wrote to warn that she will accept no refusal from me. Was that your doing, Meredith?"

She could feel the whisper of his breath against her cheek, and had to steel herself from leaning closer. "I think my mother may be the cause. She is most grateful for how you rescued me." Should she warn him about Prudence? No, that seemed unkind, and she hardly imagined Thorne would have much patience for the giggly, silly thing. "You should go, sir. It is a chance to make your way into Renwick society." And find a suitable wife, which he would soon have to do, a thought that made her stomach sink.

Thorne stepped closer. "I prefer the society I have here."

"My cousin and I can hardly be called that." Meredith met his gaze, which burned with a strange heat. "You will enjoy meeting our neighbors. I promise."

"Do you know what I would truly like?" he murmured as he looked at her mouth.

Meredith felt the touch of his breath on her lips an instant before his mouth brushed hers, and became so light-headed she clutched his arm for support. That seemed to unhinge him, for he put his hands on her waist and hauled her body against his, all the while staring down into her eyes as if he had never before seen her.

"Why do you stop?" she whispered. "I am not afraid."

His eyes glittered. "Then I must show you why you should be."

Thorne kissed her again, but this time he covered her lips and pressed his tongue between them to open her mouth. Meredith gasped, and found her mouth instantly invaded and ravished, his tongue stroking hers and pushing deep in a strange, rhythmic fashion. This carnal act further affected her body to respond in the most curious manner, sending a brandied heat through her limbs and a throbbing ache into her breasts and between her thighs. When the colonel began to touch her Meredith thought it might help, but the shocking things he did with his fingers and palms made the bizarre sensations flare up as if her body were burning from within.

Thorne had somehow tugged her bodice down around her waist, and was now doing the same to her shift. When he had bared her breasts, he tore open his shirt and pressed her to his exposed chest, so that their heated skins met and rubbed together.

"My God, you feel so good." He cupped her chin and made her look at him. "Are you afraid of me now?"

"Yes. No." She closed her eyes. "Kiss me again, please."

He seized her by the waist again, lifting her off her feet to bring her mouth to his. After another extended, deep kiss so passionate Meredith could barely breathe he hauled her even higher, nuzzling her bare breasts with his face. She tangled her fingers in his hair and thought she might faint from the sheer thrill of his closeness, and the heat of his mouth.

"We must stop," he muttered against her lips. "Or I will have you here."

A cracking sound made her peer up, and then she cried out as Thorne seized her and pushed her against the curved wall. A huge chunk of rotted wood smashed to the floor where Meredith had been standing, showering them both with shards and splinters. She stared at it as she felt her knees start to shake.

Without ceremony Thorne scooped her up in his arms, carrying her out of the tower and through the kitchen. He stopped when he reached the reception room, where he sat her down beside the fire and straightened her clothing.

"Look at me, are you hurt?" When she shook her head he pulled her close, holding her against his chest. "By God, Meredith."

The fear faded as his warmth sank into her.

"As you see, my luck never improves." She drew back and made herself smile at him. "Truly, I am well. Thank you for moving me out of the way."

"You are very pale." His mouth thinned.

"I will fetch your cousin, and some wine for the shock."

As soon as he left Meredith buried her face in her hands, her whole body trembling with reaction. His kisses had thrilled her, and she wanted more of them. To be followed by such a terrible mishap felt like a punishment for her wanton behavior. Since the rig accident nothing terrible had occurred, and she had dared to feel hopeful that nothing would again for a long time. Yet her misfortunes had followed her here, and now would ruin everything she might have had with Thorne.

You have nothing with him. He is not yours. You will never be with anyone.

Tears welled into Meredith's eyes faster than she could blink them back.

* * *

THORNE INSISTED that his steward drive them home in his carriage to give Lucetta the chance to comfort Meredith, who despite her brave face had been badly shaken by the incident. Harshad took the longer route to Starling House to allow them time to talk.

Lucetta had already seen the bruises, and the tear in Meredith's bodice, and wasted no time in demanding an explanation for them. "Meredith, I must ask you, has the colonel in any manner behaved inappropriately toward you?"

She averted her gaze. "Not in the slightest. He has been exceedingly attentive, as you have witnessed."

"What I have not seen is my concern." She hated the harshness in her voice, so she took a moment to compose herself. "I should not interfere, but my duty as your chaperone is to protect you. What happened between you and the colonel in the tower?"

"He pulled me aside to prevent me from being struck by the falling wood, just as he told you." Meredith followed her gaze and touched the darkening finger marks on her upper arm. "He was forceful, of course, but he was as surprised as I was. He did not mean to bruise me."

She sighed. "My dear, you are very young, and you have no experience with men. Please tell me the truth now. Did the colonel make any unwanted overtures? Did he put his hands on you? Is that the real reason for those marks? You can tell me the truth."

"No. Well, yes, he did put his hands on me, but only to carry me back to the reception room. I was close to swooning." Meredith reached for her mouth, only to move her hand to rub the bruises. "He is a gentleman, Cousin."

Lucetta's mouth tightened. "That is not a recommendation to me."

She said nothing more about the matter, and a short time later they reached Starling House. Harshad climbed down to help Meredith from the carriage.

"I am recovered, Mr. Naveya," Meredith told him before she gave Lucetta a wary look. "I will see you in the morning, Cousin?"

Lucetta heard the note of strain in her voice, and saw how she had twisted her hands together to conceal their trembling. She decided to indulge in another falsehood. "I am sorry, but I promised to help my brother at the parsonage tomorrow, so the next day would be better for me." That would also provide her with more time to determine what had truly happened between Thorne and her cousin.

"Of course." Meredith glanced up at the steward. "Mr. Naveya, would you be so kind as to tell Mr. Thorne I look forward to seeing him at Lady Hardiwick's assembly tomorrow night?"

Harshad nodded. "Yes, Miss."

Lucetta felt worried as she watched her cousin walk in the manor. She should return to the parsonage now, but Jeffrey and Deidre would wish to talk to her over dinner, and she needed time to sort out her thoughts. "Mr. Naveya, do you need to drive back to the hall immediately?"

"No, Miss," Harshad said as he closed the carriage door. "Do you wish to go for a drive? The road through the trees to the river has a pretty view, and very few use it."

She agreed, and felt better as he turned away from the village and drove through the woods beyond the Starlings' estate. The whole incident at the hall disturbed her deeply. Thorne had given her scant details about the mishap, and when doing so his anger had been quite visible. It seemed almost cruel that part of the tower landing should choose to fall when Meredith had just stepped inside. The bruises matched the sort of grip a man used when he didn't wish someone to escape him. The tear in her bodice suggested someone had pulled the fabric down too quickly.

The timing of the calamity seemed a little too perfect as well.

When they reached the river, Lucetta tapped on the roof, and Harshad brought the horses to a halt. She didn't wait for him to help her but climbed out and walked down to the embankment, now mostly brown with the grass that the first frost had withered. The damp, chill air slapped at her face, as if trying to pull her back from her dark thoughts. Yet Lucetta could not shake the sense that the rotten wood had not fallen by chance.

Something about Meredith's latest accident whispered of evil intent.

Her thoughts followed the path most obvious: Alistair Thorne was to blame. Why would he take her into a tower he knew to be dangerous? He knew the moment he'd offered to show it to her that she wouldn't resist; Meredith had chattered on several times about her admiration for the staircase towers.

Until today Lucetta liked Thorne, but now she wondered if her judgment had been flawed. Would the colonel have tried to deliberately hurt Meredith? For what purpose? Was he crazed? Did he take sport in tormenting the innocent? Had he caused her rig to crash to bring her under his sway?

You cannot paint every man with the same brush, her heart warned, but her head wanted no part of sentiment. She had a responsibility to protect Meredith. That came first.

Harshad came to join her, at which point Lucetta gathered her skirts and sat down. She would be sorry for that when she had to launder her gown, but just now she needed to be still and rid herself of all these unfounded suspicions. Fortunately, the steward only crouched down beside her, and said nothing. When she glanced at him she saw his dark eyes reflecting golden shards from the sun beams piercing the trees.

"You are a very good companion, Mr. Naveya," Lucetta finally said. "Most men would inquire as to why I sit here like a broody hen."

"Everyone wishes time to think," he told her as he watched the sluggishly-moving waters. "Our thoughts are all that truly belongs to us and no other, Miss."

Learning that he was a solitary soul wasn't a surprise, and yet she suspected, like her, it was not by choice. She thought of how she had felt when she had left home to take up her first position. "It must have been very difficult to leave your family behind in India."

"I did not leave them," Harshad admitted. "My parents were killed by rebels when I was a young boy. Their killers took me and my sister to Malabar, where they sold us at the slave market."

Lucetta went still. "My dear Mr. Naveya. I am so sorry that I reminded you of such a dreadful time."

"Being a slave is dreadful," he agreed. "Because I was strong for a boy of eight the man who purchased me sent me to work in his mine. Many slaves died in those tunnels, but I found an old passage they had forgot to close completely. Being small let me squeeze through it to escape. That was when the dreadful stopped."

It hurt to think of him being used so savagely, and at such a young age. "What of your sister?"

He shook his head. "For a long time, I searched for her, but I know what they do to girl slaves in Malabar. I think if she still lives, she would not wish for me to find her."

Lucetta reached out and briefly touched his hand. "I should not have pressed you for details. Please, think no more of it."

"It is good to talk with you." Harshad looked up at the sky. "Each day I wake and thank the Lord Ganesh for my freedom. Each night I kneel before the moon and ask for my sister to be blessed with the same. Do you pray, Miss Branwen?"

She wished she could, but since London she had been unable to even consider that God might exist. "I fear my faith is not what once it was."

When she tried to rise he put his hands over hers. "You have carried a burden alone too long. Share it with me. Tell me what happened in London."

"I was accused of being a thief by a man everyone believed to be respectable and trustworthy. My employer, Lord Carlton." She waited for the steward to react. "I freely admit that I stole from him, and I will never return what I took."

Harshad nodded but said nothing.

He had trusted her with his unhappy past; she could do no less. "I have always had trouble sleeping. One night I went downstairs to get a book, and heard a child sobbing. I followed the sound to one of the bookcases in his lordship's library. The crying was coming from behind it, so I found the hidden latch, pulled it open, and walked into a secret chamber there."

Harshad regarded her with sorrow in his gaze. "What did you find, Miss Branwen?"

"My employer, with one of his sons. They were both naked, and he was forcing himself on the boy, using him for his own gratification." She curled her hands into fists. "I jerked Carlton away, and took the child upstairs and locked him in my room with me. He wept in my arms all that night."

Harshad made a soft sound. "This is why he accused you of being a thief, to cover his own filthy crime."

Lucetta shook her head. "Not at first. His lordship called me to his library the next morning. He informed me that what I had witnessed was something beautiful, a love he claimed that I could not understand. He offered me a sizable amount of money if I agreed to say nothing. I did. The moment he left the house I told his wife what I had witnessed. As I suspected she knew nothing of her husband's abuse of the boy, and was horrified. I convinced her to buy passage for herself and her children on a ship to Canada, where friends of her family had settled. I gave her Carlton's bribe along with all of my savings. When it came time for them to sail, I helped them slip out of the house and accompanied them to the docks. Then I returned to the house to await his lordship. When Carlton discovered they were gone, along with all the money, he demanded I tell him everything. I refused, and he had me arrested."

"So, he thought to bully you this way," Harshad said softly.

"I did steal from him. I took his money, and his wife and children from him. He simply could not prove it without revealing his own repulsive secret." She lifted her chin and met his gaze. "As vengeance on me he made sure to ruin my reputation in London. I will never work there again."

"You sacrificed yourself to save them," he corrected softly. "This is a noble thing."

"Noble?" She uttered a bitter laugh and shoved herself to her feet. "I wanted to kill Carlton in that dreadful room, right in front of that poor child's eyes. I wanted to take up an iron from the fireplace and beat his head with it until I cracked his skull open. I am a thief, Harshad, but I very nearly became a murderer."

"You did not, Lucetta," he insisted. "You saved a woman and her children by giving all that you had."

"Including my faith in God." She took in a deep breath, and felt lighter than she had in weeks. She also realized they had been using each other's given names, something that warmed her heart. "Thank you for listening, Mr. Naveya."

He bowed to her. "It is an honor to know such a woman as you, Miss Branwen."

He walked back to the carriage with her. At the door he stopped and faced her. "My master did not make the wood fall on your cousin, or cause her rig to overturn. I know you are thinking this, but he could not do such things. He has no reason to hurt Miss Meredith. He is nothing like Lord Carlton. I swear this."

Lucetta felt astonished by how well he had guessed her thoughts. It also made her feel rather uncomfortable. Was she so easy to read? "I will trust in your faith in the colonel, then, Mr. Naveya. Please take me home now."

When they reached the parsonage, before stopping Harshad had to go around a large, grand carriage sitting directly in front of the entry. As soon as Lucetta glanced back she saw the black lion crest on the side door of the other conveyance, and her throat tightened. Lord Carlton would only have one purpose in calling on her brother.

As soon as Harshad halted Lucetta sprang from the carriage and marched up to the front door, which opened before she reached it. Her former employer, coldly elegant in pale blue and silver, stopped short as soon as he saw her. His thick lips spread into a gloating smile before he walked past her without a word.

Dread swamped Lucetta as she watched his lordship drive off. Whatever he had told Jeffrey, it would cast her in the worst light —of that she had no doubt. But she consoled herself with the knowledge that he would not have told her brother the full truth. Carlton dared not expose himself to Jeffrey as he had to her. A penniless governess's charges might be dismissed as feminine confusion or vengeance against an employer; a respectable vicar's word would carry more weight.

"Sister." Jeffrey emerged from inside, his expression bleak. "I have had a visitor and, well, we must talk now."

"Yes, I think we should." She would tell

him everything, Lucetta decided, and let him advise her as to how she should deal with his lordship. She should not tolerate any further harassment, and Jeffrey might be willing to help her seek some protection from the villain by obtaining counsel, or perhaps even taking him to court. There his lordship would not be able to tell his web of lies.

Once they had retreated to Jeffrey's study, he gestured for her to sit and went behind his desk. There he drew from an envelope a letter, which he handed to her.

"Lord Carlton has written to the bishop. It seems his family has done a great deal for the church over the years," he said slowly. "He brought a copy of the letter so that I would know its contents, and act accordingly."

Lucetta quickly read what her former employer had written. In addition to accusing her of thievery, he claimed she was an unrepentant atheist who had poisoned his wife and children with her profane notions. So damaging was her influence, in fact, that Carlton claimed his family had been torn apart by it. While her crimes might be forgiven by a loving brother, her wanton disregard for the sanctity of faith rendered her unfit to occupy the parsonage at Renwick. He implored the bishop to see Lucetta removed from the household or, if the vicar was unwilling to turn her out, to ban Jeffrey from the exercise of ministry.

"Carlton is quite convincing," she said, handing the letter back to him. "Of course, after I refused to return his property, he swore to ruin me."

"He is keeping his word, then, my dear." Jeffrey sat back and rubbed his eyes before he met her gaze. His eyelashes looked wet now. "I must ask you some questions now." His expression changed to the one he put on in front of the parish. "Are you in fact an atheist?"

Lucetta went still as what Carlton meant to do finally sank in. The letter posed a direct, serious threat to her brother's position. The church expected their vicars expected to uphold the highest standards of Christian behavior, most especially at home. By having Lucetta at the parsonage, Jeffrey would be harboring an enemy of his own faith.

Belatedly she realized she hadn't answered him. "I no longer believe in God, so yes, I am."

He leaned forward, his eyes filling with sorrow. "Did you cause this rift between Lord Carlton and his family, as he claims in the letter?"

"Not by spreading atheism, but yes, I did cause his lordship to become separated from his wife and children." She rose to her feet. "As I told you before, I also stole from him. It is all true."

If she fought Carlton on this, his lordship would not rest until her brother lost his position. Jeffrey might eke out a small living in some other, limited capacity for the church, but he and Deidre would suffer greatly reduced circumstances. He would also be forbidden from holding services or ministering to a parish. Lucetta knew that her brother's faith was more than a job, it had always been his one, true calling.

By ruining Jeffrey, Carlton would exact

a very fine revenge on her indeed. That made her decision simple.

"You need not worry about me, Brother." She smiled at him. "I will go at once."

"I would do anything for you, Lucy, you know that. But I must think of my wife, and our parish. I am first a man of God." He took from his desk drawer a small purse, which he held out to her. "This is all the money I can spare. I'm afraid it will not keep you more than a month. If you need more, perhaps–"

"I don't need it, thank you," Lucetta said before she left for her room.

Packing her few belongings took little time, and when she emerged she found her sister-in-law waiting in the hall.

"That Indian gentleman is still waiting outside for you," Deidre told her. "He refused to leave until he knew you were well, and perhaps he may... Ah, here." She handed her a satchel. "I know you do not care for my cooking, but here are some provisions. Cucumber sandwiches and apples and a bit of ham. I did not put any fruit in the scones, and the flask of tea is only once-brewed."

Lucetta's eyes stung. "I am sorry I have been such an ungrateful guest."

"You spoke only the truth." Her sister-in-law hesitated before she said, "But that Lord Carlton, he is a lying snake. May he get what he richly deserves for his wickedness." She pressed her fingers to her mouth, as if shocked by her own words. "Forgive my outburst, Miss Branwen."

"My name is Lucetta," She reached out and hugged the astonished woman, kissing her on the brow. "Thank you, Deidre."

CHAPTER 7

With tightly-leashed patience Thorne paced along the edge of the landing as the workmen carefully made their way out of the tower arch. One of them held tucked under his arm a broken, blackened board, which he presented as soon as they reached solid footing.

"Here's where that wood come from, Colonel," the carpenter said, showing him the decayed wood. "A strut under the third-floor landing gave way. What fell to the bottom broke off from this. There's naught holding it up now."

Thorne took hold of the piece, which felt disagreeably spongy and smelled of mildew. "What caused the support to snap?"

The men looked at each other before the carpenter said, "Likely the rot, sir. The top half of the stairs have begun to sag. Best to keep the servants out of here until we can clear out the punked wood and rebuild the steps."

He shook his head. "I first need the flooring in the servants' quarters replaced before the snow arrives. The tower will have to wait."

So, it had been an accident, Thorne thought as he left the workers to pack up their tools for the day. He went to the kitchen to inform his men, who had gathered there for their evening meal, that they would have to use the center staircase until repairs could be made. It was then that he noticed his steward's chair at the end of the table stood empty.

"Harshad has not returned from his rounds?" Thorne asked.

The cook started to reply, but just then the sound of a carriage came from the drive. "He has now, Master."

Outside Thorne felt surprised to see his steward helping Miss Branwen out of the carriage. "Lucetta. Is something the matter? How is Meredith?"

"She was still a little unnerved when we arrived at Starling House, but I think after a good night's rest she will recover," Lucetta said.

"I am to tell you that she hopes to see you tomorrow night at Lady Hardiwick's assembly," his steward told him.

As Thorne watched, Harshad took from the carriage one case, and then another, and a satchel after that. Lucetta removed a large hat box from the seat and added it to the pile.

Thorne regarded the baggage and then the lady. "I thought you were for home."

"I no longer have one, sir." She folded her hands in front of her, her expression strained now as she faced him. "My brother cannot offer me his hospitality and remain the Vicar of Renwick, so I have been forced to leave his house. I wonder if I might impose on your generosity again for a room tonight. I should like to speak with you, and I have no money for accommodations elsewhere."

"You are always welcome to stay."

Thorne asked Harshad to see to the bags she had brought, and escorted her to his study, where he poured them both a brandy.

"Thank you." Rather than make the usual feminine fuss over spirits she took a sip and settled back in her chair.

She appeared as exhausted as he felt, Thorne thought. "I hope your cousin has not resolved to quit Dredthorne for good."

"I insisted she stay at home for a day to rest, but I am certain she will return the next." She tucked her fist under her chin as she gazed at the fireplace for a moment. "I suppose I should explain my own situation to you."

"Your brother tossed you out, you are without funds, and you need a bed for the night." He sat down across from her and toasted her with his own drink. "I am not interested in intrigues, so that is all I need know."

"I appreciate your gentlemanly lack of curiosity, especially with my life yet again in shambles." Her gaze shifted to his sleeve, which remained pelted with wood splinters. "You desperately need a valet."

"Soldiers dress themselves," he informed her drily. "You are stalling. Whatever you wish to say, madam, out with it."

She plucked at a fold of her skirt. "My brother offered me money before I left, but I refused. He cannot afford to part with it, and I prefer to earn my way. Yet my options have become quite limited."

That was the genteel way of saying she was flat broke and had no prospects of employment, which Thorne had already guessed.

"I can certainly pay you for serving as Meredith's chaperone and helping with the books." He knew of similar arrangements among good families to provide a modest income for poor relations. "Would it not be better for you to attempt to reconcile with the vicar? Or perhaps you could stay with the Starlings."

"The most practical solution to my dilemma is to find work." Lucetta cradled her brandy between her palms. "Please understand that I have nothing but admiration for Mr. Naveya. In England, however, a man of his talents does not manage the domestics. When spring comes, your steward will be needed to attend to your financials, the property, any tenants you may wish to lease to, livestock, crops, and so forth."

"He will have no time to see to the house, then." The agent had mentioned something about such arrangements, but Thorne had been determined to do things in his own fashion. "I had not thought of it."

"It is not a criticism. A large estate like this presents many challenges for its master, and you are only just arrived. This is the first time you have had to deal with a house of this size?" When he nodded she tilted her head. "If I may ask, why have you been so determined to keep your staff wholly male?"

"I am a soldier, used to the company of men," Thorne told her, unwilling to say more than that.

"This is Renwick, not the Army, sir." She squared her shoulders. "For management of the hall and your staff, and to see to what you need to live comfortably here, you require a proper housekeeper. I propose you hire me to be yours."

Thorne had not guessed that to be her intention. "I thought you were a governess."

"My former employer has assured that I will never work as one again," she said frankly. "That comes with a great deal of very unpleasant intrigue, horror, and other matters I do not wish to discuss in detail."

He nodded. "I will not press you."

"His wishes do not remove my need of employment, and a place to live. I frequently looked after my father's household when my mother grew ill, and have worked in many large houses, so I am quite familiar with the duties. By now you are well-acquainted with my character and diligence, but if you have any questions, I am happy to answer them." She waited for him to respond, and then said, "Very well. I will accept the position for room, board, and the standard wage of twenty guineas per month, and an answer to one question."

"I have no quarrel with the amount." After watching her manage the books from the hidden library, he had no doubt she would keep the household running smoothly. All of the men liked her, and

Harshad had already befriended her. "What is your question?"

She regarded him steadily. "Did you make advances on Meredith in the tower?"

Thorne considered denying it, but saw the knowing gleam in Lucetta's eye. "Yes. I kissed her, and there was some other, ah, contact. It did not go too far."

"As housekeeper I can continue to serve as Meredith's chaperone—a role at which I warn you, I will be more diligent—and assist her with the catalog work." Lucetta made a dismissive gesture. "My own tattered reputation cannot be made worse, I assure you. Carlton has seen to that. Since I have already spent the night, and we have not fallen deliriously in love, you should be safe from your family curse."

"I beg your pardon." Fascinated now, he set aside his snifter. "My family what?"

Lucetta pressed her hand to her brow before she regarded him. "Forgive me, but I thought you knew of the legend about the Thornes. It is said that the men of your family are destined to fall in love with a lady who spends the night beneath this roof."

"How novel." He chuckled. "That does not seem to me a very great curse. Rather more a convenient one."

"The curse has to do with the lady, not the master," she said. "Once she is wed to a Thorne, the wife is doomed. Every mistress of Dredthorne is said to have gone mad, disappeared, or died within a year." She held up her hand. "I doubt its veracity, but the Thorne curse is one of the village's more enduring tales."

"It is not true." Thorne sobered as he thought of his parents. "My mother never stepped foot in this house. She met my father in London, and followed him during his naval career, which took them all over England and the Continent. They endured twenty-four years in an unhappy marriage, but they died together in an accident. I believe my father's parents also resided elsewhere, and enjoyed long, uncursed lives."

"Like most legends, this one was likely invented by a group of jealous spinsters and bored wives seething over their scandal broth." At his puzzled look Lucetta added, "Over their tea." She glanced up as the old clock chimed the half-hour, and then rose to her feet. "I must go to my room and unpack before dinner is served. Should I take the guest chamber again, or the housekeeper's room?"

"You may use the guest room." As her face fell Thorne gestured toward the ceiling. "Once the workmen have finished on the third floor, you will have the housekeeper's chamber. It comes with a sitting room, I believe."

"Thank you, sir." Lucetta bobbed in a brief, neat curtsey.

"One more thing, Miss Branwen," he said, using the more formal address. "What happened in the tower will not be repeated."

She nodded. "I will make sure of that, Colonel."

* * *

ON THE AFTERNOON before the assembly Lady Starling surprised Meredith with the gift of a new gown.

"I had planned to save it for Christmas," her mother said as she placed the jade-colored cloud of silk on her bed, "but I want you to look your very best tonight, my dear. You do not need wear that sling with it, do you? It will ruin the look, and remind everyone of your misfortunes."

"No, Mama, my arm is quite healed now." Meredith hardly knew what to say. "How in Heaven's name can we afford such a dress?"

"Do not concern yourself with matters of money," Lady Starling snapped. When she saw Meredith's expression she made an impatient gesture. "It is of no consequence. Now, I will send Annie to help with your hair after dinner." She opened the armoire. "Do you have a decent pair of slippers that will match?"

By the time her father sent for the carriage Meredith felt completely bewildered by her mother's attentions. Her hair, now piled in a clever arrangement of artful braids and curls set with Lady Starling's favorite pearl pins, resembled a gleaming crown. The gown, while a little loose around the waist, matched her eyes perfectly. Her cheeks had been pinched until they glowed, and the cherry juice she had been coaxed to sip had tinted her lips a deeper pink. Her mother had even lent her a single strand of small, creamy pearls to wear around her neck, and her favorite pair of white slippers.

Lord Starling drove them to Lady Hardiwick's himself, where they were met by Percival and Lavinia, who seemed to be waiting for them.

"By Jove, Meredith, you outshine the stars tonight," her cousin said as he helped her down from the carriage. "Careful now. Does she not look beautiful, Mama?"

"Very pretty," her aunt muttered, glaring oddly at Lady Starling. "Shall we go in, or are we to loiter here until my niece visits some new disaster on us all?"

Being reminded of her bad luck made Meredith want to climb back into the carriage, but by then Percival had tucked her arm through his, and was leading her into the Hardiwick's enormous country house.

Lamps and candles abounded on the walls, chandeliers and foyer tables, making Meredith especially nervous as she walked down the receiving line. If she caught her new dress on fire again her mother would never forgive her, and likely forbid her from ever leaving the house again.

"Chin up, Cousin," Percival said, patting her forearm. "This will be an evening to remember, I swear it."

As long as I avoid tipping the punch bowl into someone's lap, Meredith thought as she greeted their hostess.

Prudence, resplendent in a tight pink satin gown that had been cut so low the top of her breasts bulged almost to her chin, giggled at Percival's bow. She batted her eyelashes as he straightened and said, "You look so handsome in your red coat, Captain Starling."

He grinned broadly. "I am but a mere lieutenant, Miss Prudence."

"I will not tell anyone if you will not," she whispered loudly, leaning in close enough to brush the front of his jacket with her bodice. Her pale eyes shifted to Meredith. "I didn't think you'd be here tonight, Miss Fortunate." She laughed at her own joke.

"I am grateful to be included, as always," Meredith said while imagining Prudence on all fours in her expensive dress in a pen of pigs. She would likely giggle at them, too.

"Mama told me she had given that awful green gown to your poor mother," Prudence told her. "She had it made for tonight's ball, but I decided that dreadful color didn't suit me." She beamed at Percival. "Pink is my favorite color."

"It is now mine as well," he gallantly assured her.

So that explained how Lady Starling had obtained the gown, as charity from Prudence's mother. Unable to bear another moment of her simpering superiority, Meredith drew her arm from Percival's. "Please, excuse me. I must look for someone."

Dimly she heard her cousin protest, but paid no mind to it. Doubtless her mother had instructed Percival to stay glued to her side for the whole of the evening so he might rescue her from herself. Yet after what had happened in the tower she desperately wished to see Alistair Thorne. She felt sure he blamed himself for the accident, and might decide to stop her from returning to Dredthorne.

If he did, her life would quickly become unbearable.

Meredith worked her way around the edge of the ball room, watching the dancing couples in hopes of spotting the colonel. When she could not find him among the crowd, she wandered over to the refreshments table.

"Allow me," a familiar voice said from behind her as a strong hand took the punch bowl ladle from her fingers.

"I did not think you would come tonight," Meredith said, stepping to one side to allow Thorne access to the bowl. He looked exceedingly handsome in his black evening tailcoat and snowy linen cravat, tied as artfully as a Londoner's over his pale gold waistcoat. Yet all she could do as she looked at him was remember the passion of his mouth on hers. "You did not wear your uniform."

"I am no longer a soldier." Once he gave her the punch he ushered her over to a quieter spot opposite the musicians. "I hope you are recovered from yesterday's incident at the hall. I realized too late that I should never have taken you into that part of the house. The upper floors appear on the verge of collapse."

"You saved me from harm," Meredith assured him. If he was going to pretend that the embrace had never happened, then so would she. "That does not happen very often with me before some part of me is bleeding or broken. I am in your debt again."

"Here you are, Cousin." Percival abruptly joined them, followed by most of the younger girls at the ball. He regarded Thorne with a frown. "Oh, dear. I had not realized you were engaged. Forgive me if I intrude."

Meredith introduced the men before she said to her cousin, "I thought you would be occupied with Miss Hardiwick."

"She promised a dance to Travers, who outranks this lowly lieutenant," Percival said, making the girls around them giggle. "Colonel, why are you not in uniform? We must rally spirits wherever we go these days, you know. Disheartens the enemy."

"Indeed." Thorne's smile faded as he inspected her cousin's medals. "You are quite decorated for a lowly lieutenant."

"Just doing my part, sir." Percival reached for Meredith's arm. "It grows so hot in here. Come, Cousin, we will take a turn on the terrace and–"

Thorne stepped between them. "I am not finished speaking to Miss Starling, Lieutenant."

Meredith saw in his eyes the same passionate heat he'd shown her in the tower.

"I daresay this is the new master of Dredthorne." Lady Hardiwick arrived with all the pomp and ceremony of a ship sailing into port, her voluminous skirts parting the tittering girls like a sea of ribbon-sashed muslin waves. She regarded Thorne with a scowl. "Well, sir. What do you have to say for yourself?"

"Milady," Percival said quickly, "May I introduce–"

"You certainly may not." Her ladyship snapped her fan against her palm. "I am not some green girl to be made spellbound by a handsome man with a chest filled with medals. Nor do I require introductions to a person with whom I am not certain I wish to be acquainted."

"Then, my lady, I should very much like to make your acquaintance," Thorne said, and bowed. "Colonel Alistair Thorne, at your service."

"I am Lettice Hardiwick." She inclined her head a scant inch. "I thought I must send the stablemen out to Dredthorne to drag you from that French monstrosity. Indeed, why have you chosen to grace us with your presence now, when you have lived these three months like a hermit in a cave?"

Meredith closed her eyes briefly. Well, she had wished the colonel to enter society; here was the gatekeeper, demanding her due. People were starting to assemble around them to watch Thorne brace the dragon of Renwick.

"My cave has grown tiresome, my lady, and you demanded my attendance." Thorne's gaze shifted as Prudence waded her way through the girls to her mother's side. "In time I hope we may become friends."

"Do you now." Lady Hardiwick gave him a narrow look. "This is my daughter, Prudence." She hustled the girl forward and nearly sent her sprawling as she was in mid-curtsey. "Stand up straight, girl," she hissed.

"Miss Hardiwick." Thorne bowed.

"Oh, Colonel." Prudence looked all over him as she might a luscious dessert, and then indulged in the only thing she did besides giggle, which was to gush. "You are very welcome here. How do you get on with that terrible house? It is dreadfully neglected. Mama calls it a blight on the neighborhood, and Papa thinks it should be torn down. I hear you are very rich now that you have inherited, so you must spend a great deal–"

"*Prudence.*" The mention of money made Lady Hardiwick look as if she might explode.

"Excuse me, my lady, but I believe my cousin wished to dance with your daughter," Meredith said quickly, giving Percival a discreet nudge.

"Yes, for I daresay you have the bluest eyes in all of England, Miss Hardiwick." As she tittered, Percival offered his arm.

"Well done," Thorne murmured to Meredith as Prudence latched onto her cousin and steered him onto the ballroom floor, also drawing away her mother's attention.

"I should not get your hopes up, Colonel," Lady Hardiwick said, the skin around her eyes and nose wrinkling with peevishness. "Young Starling is a military hero, and quite well-liked in Renwick, unlike some gentlemen I could name." She eyed Meredith. "I am surprised you have never set your cap on your cousin, Miss Starling. For after your parents die, he will be within his rights to put you out. There will be no more cast-off dresses for you then, I daresay."

Knowing she was being punished now for interfering, Meredith smiled blandly. "I have no such expectations, my lady. Percival has always been like a brother to me."

"He is not your brother, girl. That is the material point." The older woman sniffed. "Still, I think it wise that he refrains from this hasty choice. There are many girls of very good fortune here tonight. My Prudence will make her husband a very wealthy man."

Hasty choice? Meredith had no idea her cousin had formed an attachment to any young lady.

Thorne ignored the arch look Lady Hardiwick gave him and said to Meredith. "Would you do me honor of dancing the quadrille with me, Miss Starling?"

Before Meredith could answer the older woman crowed, "Oh, no, Colonel, you can never take this girl as your partner. She is as ungainly as a cripple, particularly when she involves herself in any activity requiring grace. She could very well break your leg."

"I have survived some three hundred battles, my lady," the colonel told her. "I think I may squeak through the dangers of a country dance."

Without giving her another chance to speak he swept Meredith away to the dance floor.

"She is right, you know," Meredith murmured as she took her place in the set across from him. "No one ever wishes to partner with me."

He bowed to her along with the gentlemen in the set. "Then everyone is a fool, my dear."

For a soldier Thorne danced effortlessly, showing graceful skill that made the other men around him seem clumsy. Meredith soon forgot her nervousness and simply enjoyed the chance to spin and turn with him, clasping his hand as they moved through the steps and wove in and out of the other couples.

"I should tell you I have acquired a housekeeper," Thorne said as they waited on another couple to complete their set. "Your cousin Lucetta, as it happens."

After all the terrible questions the older woman had asked her Meredith had felt quite cross with her, but this news proved astonishing. "I do not understand. She is a governess."

"I must allow her to explain her situation to you, but we are both quite satisfied with the new arrangement." As the music slowed to an ending, he took her hand and bowed over it. "I will send her with the carriage for you in the morning, if that is acceptable?"

"Yes, of course." Meredith curtseyed in return and then walked with him from the floor. As they passed through a mass of other dancers also leaving, something caught her twisted foot and wrenched it. The pain sent her hurtling forward, her cry of alarm causing the guests in front of her to scatter in panic.

Thorne caught her before she toppled to the floor. "I have you, my dear."

Meredith looked at him and knew in that moment that no matter what her misfortunes brought on her, she would always be safe with him.

"It seems you do, sir." She glanced down at her aching foot, from which her slipper had vanished. "Only I fear I can dance no more tonight."

"Cousin." Percival rushed up, and looked at the arm Thorne had tucked around her waist. "Are you hurt? Come and sit and let me look at your poor foot. It is your foot again, isn't it? Got tangled up in your skirts?" He grimaced at Thorne. "When we were nippers she was very nearly lamed by a poacher's trap, but I saved her."

"Yes, she told me." The colonel helped Meredith hobble over to a settee, and eased her down before regarding the lieutenant.

"Perhaps you would be good enough to find her parents, so they may take her home?"

His flinty tone made Percival nod quickly and retreat. A gentleman came up and offered Meredith her missing slipper. Thorne took it from him and carefully placed it on her foot, causing some watching ladies to gasp out loud.

"This new sprain will prevent you from coming to Dredthorne tomorrow," Thorne said, and shook his head when she began to protest. "You must stay home and rest, or you will make it worse."

"I know. I did warn you this would happen," Meredith said, feeling decidedly glum. "But at least I did not tread on your feet while we were dancing."

"You did not do this," Thorn said, his voice low. "There is a tear and a scuff mark on your skirt hem, and it did not come from those white slippers. I think you were tripped. Was it that Hardiwick girl?"

"No, I caught my foot on something. The silk must have become damaged when I did." She saw her mother, father and cousin approaching and tried to rise. "I must introduce you to my parents."

"Sit down." Thorne raised an eyebrow at Percival, who quickly introduced his aunt and uncle. "A pleasure. Your daughter has been hurt."

"Yes, I see. Stumbled again, my dear? That bad foot does you ill every time. Take my walking stick." Meredith's father offered her his cane. "Are you ready to go home, my dear?"

"Yes, this night is ruined." Lady Starling looked disgusted as she adjusted her wrap. "Do enjoy yourself while you can, Colonel. Percival, give your mother our regrets, and do call on us tomorrow evening."

Meredith tried to smile at Thorne before she hobbled away after her parents, her heart throbbing as madly as her foot.

CHAPTER 8

Spending the day confined to her bedchamber allowed Meredith ample time to relive the wonderful moments she had spent dancing with Alistair Thorne. He had transformed an ever-dreaded activity into a new and exciting delight, and for once gave her a chance to be like other young ladies. If only she hadn't been so clumsy and tripped, she might have spent the evening in his company. But at least she had the memory of their one dance to cherish—and the kisses they had shared in the tower before disaster struck.

Annie brought her meals on trays, and promised to do what she could to repair the jade silk gown.

"This looks like boot blacking, Miss," the maid said, showing her the scuff mark. "You must have kicked a gentleman jolly hard to make that mark."

"I suppose I did that as I fell," Meredith told her.

As the day dragged on she thought on everything that had happened over and over. She'd felt her foot catch on something hard, something that had jerked it back and sent her off-balance. She hadn't seen what; it might have been a boot. Perhaps her foot had collided with a man's boot as he had been taking a step, but then it wouldn't have jerked backward unless he was walking past her. Everyone around her had been leaving the dance floor, moving in the same direction Meredith had been walking.

In the end she had to agree with Thorne's claim that someone had tripped her: a man, for ladies did not wear boots. But who would be so spiteful?

During her afternoon tea Meredith tested her weight on her foot, which felt much improved, and decided to go downstairs for dinner. She asked Annie to walk with her.

The last thing she needed to do was take another tumble down the stairs. But when she reached the dining room she found it empty. From there she followed the sound of her mother's voice into the sitting room.

Her mother and aunt and cousin were having a very late tea, while her father sat reading a book. All of them looked up as she came in as if expecting her.

"Mama." Meredith smiled at her cousin and aunt. "Why is everyone here?"

"I was just going to send the maid to fetch you." Lady Starling gestured for Meredith to sit beside her, a favored spot usually reserved for Percival.

"Should we not be having dinner, Mama?" she asked, feeling confused.

"We have come together for a special purpose, my dear, and had to discuss the particulars. Everything has been decided to our satisfaction." Her mother beamed happily at Percival. "Very well, my dear boy. You may proceed."

Meredith glanced up at her cousin, whom she just now realized was wearing his finest tailcoat and cravat, and then at his mother, who looked absolutely bilious. "Has something happened, Cousin?"

"Meredith, my dear girl," Percival said, placing his hands behind his back and clearing his throat several times. "You know that since we were nippers I have had much affection for you. All these years your excellent parents..." He smiled at Lady Starling. "...have treated me like a beloved son. I think I have also been of great service to you in your times of trouble."

Meredith felt a little impatient now. "Yes, I've always regarded you like a brother, Percival. I'm grateful for your many kindnesses to me." Did she have to express her gratitude every time they were together?

He frowned a little, as if she had made him lose his place in a well-rehearsed speech. "Yes, well. I know you have endured much suffering, which I find admirable. Unhappily your misfortunes have prevented any suitable man from forming an attachment to you. This has made me very sad on your behalf. Indeed, I have often wondered what I might do to assuage your pain."

"You have been a constant companion." One Meredith often wished she could avoid, truth be told. Her cousin's vanity often grew tiresome. "I daresay your brotherly affection has never wavered."

Percival pressed a hand over his heart. "Indeed, with me at your side I know I may be able to deflect future tragedy, and fill your life with new meaning and purpose."

Lavinia made a mournful sound and propped her brow against her hand.

He meant to offer for her, Meredith suddenly realized. The very notion sent a shudder of revulsion through her. Marry Percival? Allow him to kiss her and touch her and whatever more happened in a marriage?

She had to escape this before it was too late.

"I thank you for your kind words, cousin. I am feeling rather tired, so I must go back to my room now," Meredith said, rising quickly to her feet.

"Do not be ridiculous." Lady Starling tugged her back down. "You were meant to hear this last night. That was the whole reason for attending Lady Hardiwick's ball.

We intended to announce it there, before all our friends, but you spoiled that. Now permit Percival to finish what he wishes to tell you." She made an encouraging gesture to her nephew.

"I know you are in pain, dear girl, but I bring joy to you this night," her cousin assured her. "All I have ever wanted is your happiness, Meredith, and I know you feel the same. So, I have come here to ask you to join with me in the endeavor for the rest of our lives and do me the honor." He went down on one knee.

Meredith stared at his toothy smile. He really had done it. "You wish to marry me."

"Of course, he does," Lady Starling hissed.

"I am not in favor of the match," Lavinia said to no one in particular.

She looked from her cousin to her father, who seemed oblivious to what was happening. "Papa?"

Her father glanced up from his book and squinted at her. "What? Oh, yes, Percival has spoken with me, and I have given my permission." He waved a hand. "You may accept, my dear."

"I am so happy," Lady Starling said before Meredith could reply. "I never dared hope this day would come for you, and now it is here. You will remain at Starling House, and have the very best of husbands."

"Forgive me, but I will not marry Percival." As everyone stared at her, Meredith rose again. "Thank you for your offer, Cousin. I am quite conscious of the honor you do me. Yet my heart insists I speak truthfully. I am not in love with you. I absolutely cannot accept."

"What?" Lady Starling's face reddened as if slapped on both cheeks. "You may not refuse him. Tell him yes, Meredith, this very instant."

"Mama." She felt exasperated. "You cannot force me to marry."

"I am your mother, and you are very nearly a spinster. Of course, I can." Her eyes narrowed, and her jaw set. "What is the matter with you, girl? Is this how you show gratitude to a fine gentleman who has protected you, and shown you great regard, and even saved your life on more than one occasion?"

"Marriage is not about gratitude,

Mama," Meredith said quietly. "It is about sharing a life, and providing companionship, and having children together. When, or if, I do that, it will be with a man that I love."

"You need not concern yourself, my dear," her father said. "I think you still young enough to begin a family."

"I will become a grandmother." Lavinia made it sound the same as being wrapped in a shroud.

"Be quiet, Sister," her mother snapped before leaning closer to whisper to Meredith, "You are behaving disgracefully. Stop embarrassing us and accept your cousin's offer. *Now*, Meredith."

"Calm yourself, Aunt." Percival gave Meredith a narrow look, "I confess, I expected you would be more amenable to my proposal. Of course, you need time to think on it. I will call on you in a few days. Aunt, Uncle." He helped his mother to her feet and guided her out of the room, his back stiff with resentment.

Meredith felt frozen, barely hearing her mother's sharp litany of outraged rebukes. Eventually her father made a disgusted sound, closed his book and walked out, leaving her alone with Lady Starling.

"Do you care nothing for me?" she finally asked her mother, stopping her in mid-tirade. "I know I have been a trial to you and Papa, but I am your daughter. Do you truly wish me to marry a man I do not love?"

"Do you think any other man will have you?" Lady Starling demanded. "Love is a foolish girl's notion. Percival offers you his name and a home and protection. He is willing to overlook your faults, including this perpetual clumsiness that has lamed you yet again."

"No, someone tripped me last night." There, she had said it aloud. "This was not my fault. A man with black boots tried to make me fall. Annie can show you the proof."

"It is a shame he did not succeed. It might have knocked some sense into your head." Her mother stalked out of the room.

* * *

MEREDITH ROSE EARLY the next day, and

waited by the sitting room window until she saw Thorne's carriage approaching the manor. With her foot firmly wrapped she was able to walk with only a slight limp to meet her cousin at the door.

"We must go at once," she told her. "Mama is very cross with me, and if she wakes she will insist I stay home as a punishment. Possibly for the remainder of the year."

"That is cross." Lucetta helped her to the carriage, which Harshad started as soon as they were inside.

As they left Starling House Meredith let out the breath she had been holding, and regarded her cousin. She might as well tell her the rest. "Last night Percival made an offer of marriage. I refused him."

"Ah." The older woman smiled a little. "I gather your mother wished you to accept."

"She demanded I do so." Meredith described the unhappy events, and then said, "Apparently he intended to deliver his proposal at Lady Hardiwick's assembly, but I was obliged to return home early. Had I known he meant to offer for me, I would have discouraged him at once. I feel very guilty about that."

The older woman patted her hand. "Do not blame yourself, my dear. He well concealed his intentions from you."

"I should have expected it, I suppose," Meredith admitted. "He is to inherit, and my parents already regard him as a son. Yet I truly feel only sisterly affection for Percival, and he deserves a wife who can love him with all her heart." She sighed. "We are all at odds now. I fear this may be my last visit to Dredthorne Hall."

"Hold fast to your resolve, my dear," her cousin said. "In time the lieutenant will doubtless transfer his affections to another, and then your parents will have no choice but to comply with your wishes."

Meredith didn't want to think about the disagreeable situation any more. "Last night at the ball Alistair mentioned that you are to be his new housekeeper. How did that come about?"

"Quite quickly, and to our mutual satisfaction." As the carriage stopped Lucetta stiffened and leaned out to peer at a small, old rig sitting to one side of the drive.

She abruptly sighed and then met Meredith's gaze. "It seems my brother has come to call on the colonel, which is doubtless on my behalf. I will meet you in the work room shortly."

Meredith agreed, and went directly to the reception room, where she found the vicar hovering over a group of books about the history of the church.

"Good morning, Mr. Branwen." She curtseyed. "Your sister is just arrived with me."

"It is good to see you, Miss Starling." He gave her a short bow and turned as Lucetta came in with Thorne. "Lucetta, my dear. Colonel Thorne has related the news about your position here. I had hoped to have a word with you before I left."

"We will give you the room." The colonel came to Meredith and offered her his arm, and escorted her out before closing the doors. "They will likely need some time. I see you are mostly recovered from the incident at the ball. What happened has been much on my mind."

"Think nothing of it," she begged. "I daresay it helped more than it hurt."

Thorne frowned. "As you wish. Would you care for some tea?"

If this was to be her last visit to Dredthorne, she wanted to make the most of it.

"I wonder if instead I might look at one of Mr. Emerson's journals." Meredith gestured toward the hidden library. "If you do not object, that is. I have been very curious about them."

Thorne nodded, and walked with her into the dining room. "While removing the other books Harshad found the bulk of the journals are quite firmly wedged into the space, so it will take time to extract them. I have not had time to inspect those he managed to extricate. I cannot guarantee their contents will be suitable for a young lady to read."

"I am not easily shocked." After last night, she doubted she ever would be again.

He took a lamp from the table and entered the hidden library with her, where a small stack of journals sat on the desk. "Choose as you like."

Meredith took a journal from the center of the pile. When she held it up to the lamplight and opened the cover she smiled at a sketch of flowers on the first page. She showed it to Thorne. "It seems Mr. Emerson was something of an artist himself."

"Hopefully he wrote about gardening," the colonel said as they emerged from the library and left the dining room. He looked up as the sound of hammering came from an upper floor. "I must go and speak to the carpenter about a delivery."

Meredith nodded, and went past the still-closed doors of the reception room into the sitting room. She couldn't resist looking in at Thorne's study, and decided the colonel would not mind her use of it. Curling up in one of his large leather chairs, she sighed and glanced at the journal. "Well, Mr. Emerson, we are alone at last."

Meredith opened the front cover and admired the sketch again before she turned the page. The first entry, which appeared to be written in a hasty manner, had no date.

EVERY DAY I awake to the stillness and listen for

her; every night I enter my chambers expecting her there waiting. Sometimes I think I can still smell her sweet scent on my pillow in the morning, as if her ghost comes to lay with me when I sleep. Why did I continue to build a mansion for a dead wife? Have I finally gone mad?

"POOR MAN." Meredith gnawed at her lower lip as she turned the page to find a sketch of an older woman with kind eyes surrounded by blooming roses.

On the facing page, Emerson Thorne had written more.

SHE IS everything I see and smell and think and dream now, but the pain ebbs with each new dawn. I have done right to come here; more flowers appear in the garden each day, as if to keep me company. I think she may be sending them to me from Heaven.

"HOW LOVELY." She settled back to continue reading, and sighed as the next pages described in detail every bloom the old man saw, with detailed sketches of each. He wrote under them the names he knew, but then he began giving them more fanciful titles and wrote of what he regarded as their personalities.

WHEN IT IS QUIET, Frost Rose peeks at me through the bed of new violets. Her face is all white flounces and dewy lace, and in her center, a purely golden heart. She seems to be waiting for me to appear with my tea every morning, and we are good company together.

Prince Hyacinth thrusts his pikes of blue and purple bells toward the heavens, and his scent is as mighty as his colors. Was his namesake killed by the great god Apollo, as myth would have it? I know no bloom as bold or commanding.

And then the crimson trumpets of Harlot Hollyhock draw my eye. She is all crimson in her gaudy display, almost taunting as she reminds me that I will never again know the joy of passion. I would hate her, were she not so correct in how she judges me.

I stay longer and longer in the gardens each

day, and soon I think I must bring some of the flowers into the house with me, and plant them about my bed, that I may sleep and dream of my lost beloved.

TO THE NEXT PAGE A PRESSED, dried rose had been fixed, so ancient now it began to crumble the moment Meredith exposed the page. She quickly turned it over to find a very different passage written in a bold, slashing hand.

HE TOOK HER FROM ME, but I cannot prove it. I only know it in my heart, as surely as I know his rage at being denied his prize. I saw him yesterday in the village, and the smirk of satisfaction he gave me told all. I went directly to the magistrate, but he insists grief has addled me. He will not believe that my wife was murdered by that gloating villain. They are good friends, so I know he is protecting him.

What am I to do without recourse? I dare not seek satisfaction by challenging him, for he is renowned for his prowess with the sword. Even if I were fortunate enough to land a lethal blow before he could slay me, I have heard the whispers among the servants. His family has sworn themselves my enemies. They should never allow me to live.

I must take solace from being the means of his ruination.

Appalled by the disturbing confession, Meredith quickly turned the page, only to find it had been torn out. What followed that were pages of plans for Dredthorne Hall's gardens, written in dull, dry terms with no further mention of the terrible crime Emerson Thorne had suspected, or the name of the man he blamed for murdering his wife.

She could show this to her cousin and the colonel, but what could be done? If the lady had been murdered a century past, then her killer would no longer live. *Perhaps this was what founded that dreadful legend about the Thorne family curse.*

"Here you are," Lucetta said as she came into the study, her face slightly flushed and her tone fraught with agitation. "I have finished bickering with my dear brother, who is reassured I am not casting myself to the wolves here. Other matters, well, they have resolved themselves. Shall we have some tea before we begin the work?"

"I would like that." Meredith took the journal and placed it on Thorne's desk. Since the entry involved his ancestor, he would have to decide who, if anyone, should know about it.

THE REVELATION of Emerson Thorne's suspicions lingered in Meredith's thoughts all morning, distracting her. Despite her determination to carry on with the cataloging, Lucetta kept rubbing her temple and seemed unable to concentrate on the notations she had been writing. At last she put down her quill and sighed.

"I fear I cannot think with this headache." She grimaced. "Would you mind terribly if I retreat to my room? A cold compress and some rest should cure it."

"Allow me to help you upstairs." Meredith started to rise, subsiding as

Lucetta made a staying gesture. "Are you certain? I would not mind sitting with you."

"I am better left alone just now." The older woman smiled before she retreated.

Meredith glanced down at the short list of titles she had written, but instead saw the terrible words from the journal entry. She should find the colonel and tell him what she had discovered now, while Lucetta was resting.

She closed the ledger and went to retrieve the journal from Thorne's study, but when she approached the desk she saw no sign of it. Frowning, she went around and bent over to see if it had fallen.

"Meredith?"

She straightened without thinking, and banged her head on the edge of the desk. Clasping a hand to the sore spot, she squinted at Thorne, who was striding rapidly toward her. "Alistair. I came to retrieve the journal I was reading earlier, but it has vanished."

"Come here." He guided her to the chair by the fire and moved her hand away to inspect her scalp. "I am sorry I startled you." He placed the journal in her hands. "I found it when I came down to retrieve some plans."

She opened it and showed him the entry written after the page with the rose. "You should read this."

Thorne frowned as he did. "This is quite unsettling."

"I did not show it to Lucetta." Meredith watched him skim through the following pages. "That appears to be the only entry he wrote about the matter. I thought since it concerned your family that I should say nothing until we spoke."

"I am not certain what to make of it," he said gravely as he closed the journal. "It seems obvious that my ancestor wished to place blame for the loss of his wife. Grief can make a man irrational. Yet he seems quite convinced." He looked into her eyes. "I should have read it first."

She felt miserable for him and herself. "I fear I have more unhappy news. After today my parents may not permit me to return to Dredthorne. They are quite put out with me for refusing to marry Percival."

He turned away, but said nothing.

"I really do not wish to end a spinster,"

she said quickly to fill the awful silence hanging between them. "I would like to have children, and a good home, and a husband. I have known Percival all of my life. Do you think I should accept his offer, Alistair?"

"If you love him, yes." He sounded angry and sad at the same time. "You deserve to be happy, Meredith."

She had hoped he would demand otherwise. She had yearned for him to offer to be her happiness. "It is only that I cannot be a wife to him. I could never do with Percival those things that…that wives do with husbands."

"I think you should speak about this to your mother," he said stiffly, still not looking at her.

"She will not listen to me," Meredith said, rising from the chair and walking back and forth in front of the hearth. "She does not care what I want."

Thorne turned and stared at her. "And what do you want?"

You. But I cannot have you.

"Wifely affection," she blurted. "I can

never feel that for Percival. Marrying him will not change my feelings at all."

"I see." Thorne moved away from her to stand at the windows, where he stared out at the back terrace. "Might I call on them and persuade them to–"

Whatever he meant to say was interrupted by a sudden billow of flames and smoke from the fireplace. Embers pelted Meredith's skirts, which caught fire as she stumbled away from the hearth. *"Alistair."*

CHAPTER 9

Thorne tore the drapes from the window and engulfed her in them as he hauled her away, using the heavy material to smother the flames crawling up her skirts. Once he was certain they were extinguished, he picked up a fire bucket beside the hearth and doused the smoldering carpet with sand before returning to her to check her dress again, which no longer burned.

"I am truly cursed," Meredith said, her face so white it looked carved from chalk. Her eyes rolled up in her head and she dropped.

Catching her, Thorne carried her out of the study and upstairs. He only realized he had brought her to his bed chamber when he placed her on the silk coverlet. He called her name, but she did not stir, and she barely breathed.

Thorne had seen the shock of sudden injury kill soldiers, and frantically ripped open her bodice and dragged her scorched gown from her still form. He saw no burns, thankfully, only soot marks on her skin transferred from the fabric. He removed the dagger from his boot and used the blade to slice through her stays. Some color returned to her face as the release allowed her to breathe more naturally.

Once he had her swaddled under the blankets on his bed he tore off his own soiled jacket and shirt and stretched out beside her. Gathering her against his chest, he tucked a leg over hers and warmed her with the heat of his body.

"You must wake up, Meredith." He looked down at her face and lifted a hand to stroke a tangle of hair back from her brow. "I have not yet shown you the rest of the house. You wished to see every room, did you not? And climb to the top of both towers to see the view. So, you will, just as soon as I have the steps made safe."

She did not move or respond, but the weak patter of her heart seemed to him stronger now.

"Over the last day I have received a dozen new invitations," he murmured, pressing her cheek to his own hammering heart. "Including another ball at Christmas. You must reserve two dances for me. I have never enjoyed dancing as much as I did with you."

She did not stir, but Thorne could feel the tension easing from her limbs. He thought he saw a tear on her cheek, but when he wiped it away he found it to be a shard of glass. He thought of the suddenness of the explosion of fire. If he went back to the study now, he felt certain he would find more shards of glass.

Someone had dropped a lamp down the chimney, which had smashed and caused the blast. Someone had done this to hurt her.

Thorne wanted to find the man responsible, and beat him to death. Instead he kept talking nonsense to Meredith, knowing the sound of his voice might draw her back to her senses. When she did not rouse, he pulled her close and held her tightly.

"Listen to me now, my girl. I know you are frightened and weary. So am I." He pressed his lips to her brow, "I have felt just the same every day since leaving India. But you cannot surrender, Meredith. You must fight this, and come back to me. We will find the one who has done this, I promise you. Together."

"Alistair."

The barest whisper of his name came with a soft puff of breath against his chest.

"Meredith?" He gazed down at her, and cradled her face between his hands. "Say that again. Say my name. Please."

"Alistair." Her eyes fluttered and then slowly opened, and she shook her head a little. "Why?"

"Someone tried to hurt you, my dear," he told her. "I put out the flames. You are not burned."

"No. That is not what I mean." She

glanced down at his bare chest, and the thin chemise covering her breasts. "Why are we here, like this?"

He drew back a little. "You suffered a bad shock, and could not breathe. I had to remove your stays and warm you. Lying together in this fashion is the most effective means."

"Oh." She nestled back against him. "That was very good of you." She peeped up at him, her expression uncertain. "I fear I cannot tell Dr. Mallory about this method when he returns from his journey. I think he would not approve."

Thorne sighed his relief; she had come back to her senses. "Yes, and he would relate it to your parents, who would most certainly regard it unfavorably." He lifted his hand to stroke her cheek. "Meredith, someone has been tormenting you by arranging these mishaps and accidents. Now I am convinced of it."

"You think to find someone in your chimney? The mysterious gentleman who tripped me at the ball, perhaps?" She shook her head. "I am cursed, Alistair."

"As it happens, so am I." He pulled her closer so that her soft breasts pressed against the vault of his chest. "Look at me now. There is no curse. Why do you frown?"

"We should not be in this bed together," she whispered as she stared at his mouth. "Although I never want to leave it. I have fallen in love with you."

He groaned as she pressed her cheek to his shoulder. "Now I never will."

"I did not mean to love you," she told his shoulder. "I was quite happy being a spinster, you know. Then my rig overturned and you were there and I was lost." She hesitated before she added, "I should confess something. I know nothing about this, truly. Mama would never tell me."

Thorne knew she was warm, and that he should release her and leave her to rest. He also knew there was no force in Heaven or on Earth that could make him do so. "Do you wish me to tell you what they do?"

She bit her lower lip. "I would very much like you to show me."

"So would I, more than I can tell you." He picked up her hand and held it between his. "Meredith, I would happily spend the rest of day and night here with you in my bed. But that cannot happen. I would not stop at kisses and caresses. What I do want could cause you to have a baby."

She stared at him. "I thought a woman had to be first married in order to be so blessed."

He shook his head. "Children are made by men and women in bed, as we are, and they do not have to be married to be together in that manner."

She pressed her palms over her eyes. "You must think me a complete simpleton."

Thorne drew her hands down. "Most young ladies are not informed on such matters until their wedding is imminent. When my own mother was told the night before her ceremony, she claimed she nearly called it off."

"I would not," Meredith told him. "If we were to be married...not that I would expect...oh, I am such a turnip-head."

"You are wondrously sweet." He smiled a

little, until she pulled him on top of her. "Meredith."

"I have not changed my mind." She parted her legs to make room for him between them. "I am in love with you, sir. Would you be so kind as to show me *all* I should know?"

"Very well." Thorne covered her left breast with his big hand and felt her catch her breath. "We must start by removing the last of our clothing."

* * *

THE SCENT of flowers woke Lucetta, who opened her eyes to see a bouquet of wildflowers sitting on the table beside her bed. The colors of the last of the autumn blooms glowed in the late afternoon sunlight. That they had been left for her while she had been sleeping did not disturb her as much as whom she believed placed them there.

Somehow Harshad Naveya always knew what she needed to hear. Now, apparently, he sensed what she needed to see. Soon he would be reading her every thought, and she could not bear that.

Lucetta rose and tidied herself before going downstairs. She found the reception room empty, so it seemed that Meredith had gone home. She had only herself to blame for that, but it could not be helped. Now her cousin would be trapped in that aging manor with a mother insisting on her marrying that dunce of a nephew. It seemed utterly ridiculous.

She walked out onto the back terrace, and made her way down the steps to walk along the old garden beds. She knew she should return and check on the preparations for dinner, but the cook likely had that well in hand. She kept walking as she realized that as part of the staff she would be expected to eat in the kitchen with the rest of the servants. She would not mind that; she liked the men.

Lucetta walked until she reached a meadow that had not yet browned, tucked in the midst of an elm grove. She looked around her with some confusion and realized she could no longer see Dredthorne Hall. She had not meant to wander so far from the house. Tired of walking, she sank down onto the grass.

"Miss Branwen?"

She glanced up as Harshad Naveya's graceful form approached. Some of his black curls had escaped his queue, and gleamed like spun onyx on his shoulders. "Mr. Naveya."

Instead of offering her a hand up he knelt down in the grass before her. His dark gaze shifted to the flowers she held and then returned to her face. "You have been crying."

Had she? Lucetta touched her cheeks, astonished to find them wet.

"I lost my handkerchief." She bowed her head. "Thank you for the flowers, Mr. Naveya. They are lovely, but I do not deserve such attention."

"I thought they would make you smile." He held out a folded square of colorful cloth. When she did not take it, he added, "It is not soiled, Miss Branwen."

"I do not doubt that. You are the cleanest man of my acquaintance." She took it as if it were made of silk, and used it to blot the wetness from her cheeks. "May I call you by your given name while we are alone?"

"You already have before now, Lucetta," he chided.

"Harshad, you have been very kind to me, and I thank you for it." Speaking firmly came naturally to her, so she should have no trouble with the rest. "It is unseemly for you and I to be friends. I am the housekeeper, and you are the steward. We must refrain from any future expressions of affection. It is not proper."

He looked all over her face. "What did your brother say to you to make you troubled and angry?"

Lucetta abruptly got to her feet and stalked away from him.

A hand encircled her wrist and pulled her around to face Harshad. "It was Lord Carlton again. What has this man done now?"

She saw the burning in his eyes, the same that blazed in her heart, and she placed her pale hands on his dark face. "Oh, my dear friend. You mistake my anger. It is for myself. Lord Carlton can do nothing more to anyone. He is dead."

Lucetta turned to walk back to the hall, but her feet would not obey her. Harshad came to stand beside her, saying nothing at all. Then the words just seemed to spill from her lips.

"It seems that Lady Carlton wrote from Canada to everyone she knew—family, friends, and neighbors—and she informed them of what her husband had done to their son. She also revealed how I helped her escape with the children. The letters arrived just as Lord Carlton returned to London. Everyone knew." She closed her eyes for a moment. "As soon as he learned he had been exposed, his lordship went home and hung himself."

Harshad made a soft sound. "You are free now, Lucetta."

"Yes, and my good name has been restored. Since she did not know my whereabouts, Lady Carlton wrote to my brother. She is arranging for her family to repay the money I gave her for their passage." Her knees wobbled and she fell to them. "I am glad he is dead. I am glad, do you hear? I wanted to laugh and dance and go to London and spit on his grave. What does that make me?"

Harshad knelt before her, and touched his brow to hers. "You saw a terrible thing. You chose to save the child. Lucetta, you ruined your life to save them all." He softly pressed his mouth to her right eyelid, and then her left. "You are blessed in the eyes of God."

"I don't believe in God anymore," she whispered.

"I will believe for both of us." His mouth touched the corner of hers.

In possibly the most wanton, reckless and wholly natural impulse of her life, Lucetta turned her face so that her lips were on his. For a moment Harshad went still and then his arms were around her, pulling her against his hard body, his fists bunched in the back of her dress.

Lucetta had no knowledge of passionate kisses, but Harshad quickly educated her with his lips and tongue and even his teeth. He kissed her as if he wished to do nothing else for the rest of his days, openly, wetly, as if starved for such a thing. She behaved in much the same manner, at first a bit awkwardly, but the delight and heat that billowed inside her soon swept away those girlish feelings and brought her into panting, full-blown womanhood.

"My sweet," he gasped after he wrenched his mouth from hers. "We must stop this now."

"Absolutely not," she snapped, tangling her fingers in his curls. "You will kiss me again, and again. That is what I want. And you, you want it just as much."

"I am a man." He dragged her hand down to the front of his trousers and pressed it over the long bulge beneath the rough fabric. "I want to join with you. Put myself, put this, inside your body."

She would let him do anything he liked to her, but having a baby out of wedlock would bring shame on their child. "We will have to marry before we do that."

His expression cleared. "Yes, please. I would like that very much."

Lucetta felt hot and faint as she slowly rubbed her palm over the ridge of his erect manhood. "I can tell."

"Now I am blessed by God." He spread his hand over her lower belly, and rubbed her there with the same, slow deliberation. "We could marry very soon?"

She took a note from his book and said, "Yes, please."

* * *

THANKS TO NOVELS, Meredith had some notion of what she had asked of Alistair. As he undressed them both she knew it felt very different from reading words in books. Pinned beneath his large, heavy form made her feel hot, but not from the weight or press of it. No, this was more an internal burning, kindling upon waking in his arms, and flaring from the moment he placed his hand on her womanly curves.

Breast, she thought, correcting herself. *That is my breast he caresses now. And he likes it. He keeps looking at it in an admiring fashion.*

"Meredith."

She glanced up at him, suddenly aware of how fiercely she was concentrating. "Yes, sir?"

"We do not have to do this now." His voice sounded gentle and yet somehow strained. "We could delay it until we have had more time to…discuss such matters. Perhaps even become engaged."

He was trying to be kind to her, again, and suddenly Meredith could not bear it. "Colonel Thorne, I am naked, in your bed. I am not interested in discussing this or the possibility of marriage. That can come later. What I wish to do now is make love. Now, if you please."

"I am at your command, my dear." He smiled a little. "We will begin with our mouths. You know how this is done. Part your lips for me."

As soon as Meredith did so, he put his mouth over hers in an open kiss, and pressed his tongue between her lips. The sensation felt even more delicious than the first time he had kissed her, likely because she enjoyed the gliding strokes, the taste of his mouth, and the rumble of sound he made in his chest.

Alistair lifted his head. "You may do the same to me now, if you wish."

Meredith nodded, and reached up with her mouth, somewhat awkwardly imitating the kiss he had given her. He sucked on the end of her tongue lightly as she did, sending a peculiar burst of sensation into her breasts.

"Oh, dear." She glanced down. "Something is amiss with me."

He looked at her breasts, which appeared flushed and somewhat swollen to Meredith. The oddest aspect was how her nipples had changed. The soft rosy tips had turned a darker color and contracted as they sometimes did when she was chilled. They also ached with something like pain that was perversely almost pleasurable.

"You are becoming aroused," Alistair murmured to her. "Desire causes this, and when it engages our senses our bodies change. Women show very subtle but definite signs of sexual arousal. As you have noticed, your nipples grow hard. You may also feel a dampness between your thighs."

"Indeed." She felt utterly fascinated. "How does a man's body change?"

"In far more flagrant fashion." He moved against her so that she felt the hard length of him against her folds. "What you feel is my cock. When I am aroused, it becomes erect, so that I may penetrate you."

So that was what he would put inside her body, as the animals did. Meredith had suspected as much, although she had not anticipated his cock would be quite so large. "Does this happen now?"

"Sometimes, if the man and woman have great need." He cradled her breast in his hand. "We have no reason to hurry. This is your first time, my lovely girl, and I want to make it memorable."

"I should like that." She cleared her throat. "Do you mean to kiss and fondle me before we attempt these other matters, sir?"

"I should like to, very much." Thorne brushed his thumb over her pebbly nipple. "This part of you wants to be kissed and fondled, and suckled, does it not?"

The thought of Alistair's mouth on her breast made Meredith feel a little dizzy. "I believe it might, sir."

"You will watch me do this to you," he said before he lowered his mouth and enveloped her nipple. At the same time his hand began gently squeezing the mound of her breast around it.

The feel of his tugging and suckling caused Meredith to shiver violently, and now she could feel a definite wetness down there. She had seen mothers in the village nursing their babies in such fashion, of course, but the sight of Alistair sucking at her breast engendered far fewer tender feelings. On the contrary, at present she thought she might shriek out with crazed need.

Alistair lifted his head and moved his mouth to her other breast. Before he touched it, he said, "Tell me what you feel when I do this to you, Meredith."

"I feel very heated inside," she admitted, and took in a sharp breath as he commenced with licking and sucking and fondling. "The wetness you spoke of is becoming most pronounced. I want something, quite desperately, but I do not know what it is, exactly."

He made a rough sound and rolled his hips against hers, again stroking her most intimate place with the long, thick shaft of his penis.

"Oh, Alistair." Something down there sent a jolt of aching pleasure through her. "Do that again, please."

He did so, and then took his mouth

from her breast and watched her face as he reached down between them with his hand. "You may enjoy more direct stimulation for now."

"What are you doing.. Oh," she gasped as she felt his fingers parting her folds. "You are fondling me down there?"

"Yes. I very much want to touch you between your legs." He used his fingers to probe and stroke her. "Does this feel good to you?"

"I...I'm not certain." She felt entirely wicked now for permitting him to intimately caress her in such a private place. "Your fingers are becoming very wet from me."

"That is to be expected," he assured her. "I enjoy the feel of any part of you on my skin. Such contact makes my cock cry for you."

This revelation astounded her. "It weeps?"

"Yes." His eyelids drooped and his voice went low and soft. "Put your hand on me and you will feel it."

She raised her brows. "I am permitted to touch you as well?"

He chuckled. "You may touch me and kiss me and do anything you please with me, Meredith. Anywhere."

"May I look upon you, then?" She felt brazen for asking, but he had given her permission to do as she wished. "I have never seen a man unclothed."

Alistair drew back the covers, rather slowly, Meredith thought. Likely he expected her to be shocked or scream or have the vapors, or perhaps all three. But as he exposed his body to her, she found the only difficulty she had was with breathing properly.

"Oh, my." She admired the hard-muscled planes of his chest, and the flat narrow span of his belly, but it was his erect manhood springing into view that held her utterly riveted. "Alistair." She reached out and gently touched the shaft with just the tips of her fingers before meeting his narrowed gaze. "You are made so very large."

"Desiring you makes me thus." His eyes shifted to the other half of the covers that still draped her. "May I look upon you as well?"

"I am nothing to you," she warned him, "but yes, if you wish."

"I think you are mistaken." Alistair slowly exposed her naked form, his hand returning to caress the small, hard mounds of her breasts. "Yes, here is the evidence. These are quite lovely."

"My mother thinks I am rather small-bosomed," she said. "But I rather like them. They should never pop out of anything, which pleases me. I do not care for larger ladies who so often tempt Fate with the depth of their necklines. May I put my hand on you again?"

He traced a circle around one of her nipples and sighed. "If you do, I may disgrace myself."

Meredith frowned at him. "Have we not both done so thoroughly already?"

"I meant, I may lose control and spill my seed on your hand," he clarified. "Your touch is somewhat unbearably arousing, my dear."

"Good." She ran one hand over his broad shoulder. "It means we are well-suited. for yours does the same to me."

"If I spill, I cannot proceed with the rest

of what you have asked me to show you," he warned. "At least, not immediately."

"Oh. I shouldn't want to delay." In fact, she did, but not to his detriment. "I may touch you again later, when your needs are not so urgent?"

"Yes." He rolled on top of her again, his weight and nakedness sending shivers through her.

Meredith parted her legs to make room for him there, and felt the bulbous end of his shaft rooting against her. "There is a great disparity of sizes, sir. I do not think that part of you will fit it where it is meant to go."

"That is why you are wet, love," he murmured, reaching down between them and grasping his shaft to seat it more firmly against her. "So that I may come into you, where I long to be." His expression grew serious. "There may be some discomfort, this first time."

"Because I have never been with a man," she guessed, and he nodded. "Will it hurt very much?"

"It is different with every woman," he admitted. "But those who are eager, who welcome it, seem not to mind so much." He took her hand down between them, and curled her fingers around his shaft. "We will do this together, love."

Her hand tightened. "Yes."

Meredith felt his hips move over hers, and the plum dome pushed between her nether lips, stretching them as he penetrated her. She felt no pain, and once the head lay fully inside her body the wetness encompassed it.

"Look at me," Alistair murmured, and when she did he pushed again, this time sending the hard column of his manhood much deeper. "What do you feel?"

"It doesn't hurt." She wriggled under him. "It feels as if it should be there. Oh." A frisson of sensation swept over her as he forged ahead, sinking his penis so deeply in her that their netherhair meshed. "You are so big, Alistair, yet we fit so well together. I must have space in there of which I am not aware."

"There is no space between us." He drew back and then penetrated her a second time, the motion definite, and the friction delightful. "You are squeezing me with your tightness."

Just as he was stretching her with his girth now. "Does it hurt?"

He put his mouth to hers and gave her several urgent thrusts of his tongue before he replied. "It is the sweetest pain a man can ever know." He pushed her legs up, bending her knees and spreading her thighs wider. "I want to fuck you now, Meredith. Will you have me?"

The forbidden word made her gasp, but the movement of his shaft inside her was too wonderful to deny. "Yes, please, Alistair."

He cradled her hips with his hands and set at her, pushing deep inside her quim with his swollen cock, dragging it back out until only the pulsing head lay within. He repeated these actions over and over, his body coiling and recoiling over her.

Meredith soon felt her breasts bounce with the strength of his thrusts, and now and then he would put his mouth to them to suckle her again. The sensation added to the act and began something inside her, causing her to arch under him and writhe as she tried to resist it.

"No, love, don't fight it," he panted as he thrust and withdrew. "What you feel is pleasure. Give yourself to it. Give yourself to me, Meredith."

She wanted to tell him she did not know how to do so, and then she was exploding from within; her body convulsing beneath his as a hot, sweet delight billowed through her.

"Yes, yes," Alistair said, his voice hoarse and shaking now, and as a second conflagration gripped her he pressed deep, his shaft swelling and then pulsing as a warm wetness flooded her clenching tissues.

Meredith pulled his head down and cradled it against her breast, holding him as he shuddered through his own pleasure. She had never felt such emotion, her desire for him easing into a tenderness so acute it brought tears to her eyes.

He lifted his head, easing himself from her body and rolling to one side. She turned to face him, and his big hand caressed her cheek.

"And that is the way of men and women," she whispered, entirely enchanted.

"Naked together, in bed, and wanting each other," he replied, bringing her hand to his lips. "That is how I will always want you now."

"Then we should talk about marrying later." Meredith nestled against him and closed her eyes, drifting into peaceful bliss.

In the dark, Thorne could not find his friend.

"Nigel?"

All around him echoed the savage sounds of butchery, the cries of fallen men and the gruesome shouts of the advancing rebels. Blood soaked his uniform, and dripped from the gash on his brow into his eye. His hand shook as he swiped at the burning crimson tears. He fell and then pushed himself up from the dirt, unwilling to surrender himself to the pain and the blackness waiting beyond it.

A terrified lieutenant staggered up to him. "Colonel, they are too many. We must– *Ah*." He toppled over, a huge curved sword buried in his back.

In the madness of battle Thorne fought his way toward the small knot of officers desperately trying to hold their position. He could see rebels coming from all directions around them, and only a narrow avenue of escape.

Men fell all around him as a heavy weight bore down on his shoulders. It felt crushing, and yet he knew he had to bear it. It was Nigel, and he needed help. Thorne put one foot in front of the other. He had only a few moments before they would cut him down. Something jabbed him in the back, and he staggered, sure he would fall.

He could not fall. If he fell, they both would be killed

"I am here, Alistair," a low voice said from the darkness. "Come back to me now."

"Nigel." The weight vanished as he spun around, peering through the shadows at the blurry pale face of his captain. "There are too many. We are overrun. The general has sounded retreat. I cannot see– No." He tried to push his friend away. "We must go. Run. That way. They will kill you. Hurry, Nigel."

Soft, cool hands touched his wet,

burning face. "Alistair, look at me. Look. It is Meredith."

Thorne jerked upright to find himself standing naked in his darkened chamber. He stared at Meredith, who stood in front of him, her lovely eyes filled with worry. The memories of the terrible battle, and the relief to find himself alive, flooded him with the despair he had never been able to escape. He pulled her into his arms and held her as he tried desperately to compose himself.

"You were shouting in your sleep," Meredith murmured to him. "I could not rouse you from the nightmare."

"How long has it been?" he asked her, glancing at the darkened window. He could see the moon rising. "It must be the middle of the night."

"It does not matter." She smiled. "We were both exhausted. Come back to bed now."

"I cannot." Thorne jerked on his breeches and looked for his dressing robe. "Go to sleep, my dear. I will take you home in the morning."

She sank down on the bed. "You are leaving me alone?"

Meredith sounded so forlorn he dragged a hand through his hair. "I have an affliction that prevents me from sleeping properly. I am plagued by nightmares. They cause me to sleep walk as I just did. I do not wish you to see me like this."

She held out her hand to him, and when he took it drew him down beside her. "That is why you always look so weary. You cannot sleep. What causes these terrible dreams?"

He should not tell her anything, but she had already seen the worst of it.

"My regiment was ambushed, and massacred by rebels. I was the only survivor." Thorne brought her hand to the scar hidden by his hair. "When retreat was sounded, I carried my best friend, Major Nigel Robbins, from the battlefield. He was badly wounded, and could not walk. I was attacked from behind again and again, but somehow I did not fall. I refused to stop. Nigel was already dead by the time I reached help. Then I nearly died myself.

Those terrible hours, all the effort I spent trying to save him, unaware that he was already gone… That is what I dream of, every time I close my eyes."

"Oh, my love." She leaned against him, and stroked her fingers gently against the old wound. "I am so sorry."

"That is why I avoid this bed." Thorne laced his fingers through hers. "This has been the most peaceful night I've had since my return to England, and you saw how that ended." He kissed her brow. "I will leave you to your rest." He rose, but stopped short as she held onto his hand. "Meredith, you can do nothing about this."

"I can hold you in my arms," she told him as she drew back the coverlet. "I can wake you from the nightmare, and hold you again until you calm. Please let me try."

"I have become violent in the past, believing myself to be in battle," he told her flatly. "I might harm you. That is why I have never wanted women in this house. A man can stand up to another man, especially one gone crazed. A woman…" He shook his head.

"I am not afraid," Meredith insisted. "You do not have to bear this alone, Alistair."

Joining her on the bed felt more like a victory than a surrender. Thorne wrapped his arms around her, and held the slender softness of her body close.

"You are mad, you know," he told her. "I am not exaggerating about my affliction. When I sleep-walk I am unaware of what I do. I could attack you and never know it."

"I will wake you, and you do not have any weapons." She lifted the coverlet to look under it. "Well, there is that. But I like that very much."

The laugh that came from him sounded rough, almost torn, but it felt good. He pulled her close, and let himself relax.

"Would you tell me about your friend Nigel?" Meredith asked after a time. "Before the battle, did you spend much time together?"

"We were inseparable." Thorne smiled a little. "He was a fine soldier, but the best of men. He always knew how to keep the troops in good spirits, charm the natives, and even befriend some of the monkeys that would plague the camp. I never knew him to be cross or disagreeable. He looked upon every day as a new adventure, every campaign as an exciting journey."

He related to her the time when Nigel had gotten lost in a market while purchasing tea and other supplies for their men. None of the vendors spoke English, and had little love for British soldiers. Yet without speaking a word of Hindi, Nigel managed to convince some raggedly-dressed children to lead him out of the confusing maze of stalls and tents, and then rewarded each of them with a guinea, emptying his own purse.

"He beggared himself for beggar children," Thorne said. "It seemed foolish, but I secretly envied him his gallantry. I think all the officers did."

"Just as you were gallant when he fell injured," Meredith said softly. "You tried to save him, Alistair. He died knowing that."

Thorne had only ever dwelled on his failure to save his friend. He had never once considered what Nigel might have thought of his efforts. "I often wished that I had died, and he had lived, because he was the better man."

"If he had, I think Captain Robbins would wish the same." She lifted her head to gaze into his eyes. "You tell me I must not blame myself, and yet you do the same thing."

Thorne pulled her close.

"You are right," he murmured against her hair. "And you are marrying me, my dear, just as soon as we may arrange it. Now, about my one weapon..."

* * *

MEREDITH ROSE at dawn and borrowed Thorne's dressing gown before she glanced at her sleeping lover. He had barely moved for hours, so deep was his slumber, and she suspected he wouldn't wake for some time yet. She slipped out of the chamber and walked down the hall to Lucetta's room, taking a deep breath before she gently tapped on the door.

Her cousin opened it and said, "I will be down for...*Meredith*." She looked over her and took a step back. "You did not leave yesterday."

"No, I stayed the night." She smiled. "With Alistair. In his bed."

Lucetta hauled her into the chamber and shut the door. She started to say something, closed her mouth, walked across the room, came back and pressed a hand to her forehead.

"I am not ruined, exactly," Meredith assured her.

Her cousin peered at her as if she had gone mad.

This was not proceeding as well as she'd hoped. "The colonel has asked me to marry him. Well, he told me that I am marrying him, but I am in agreement. There was also a small fire that burned my gown. Might I borrow one of yours before I go home to tell Mama and Papa? They will take the news better if I am dressed."

Her cousin blinked. "A fire?" When she nodded she went to the closet and began looking through the gowns hanging inside. "Meredith, start from when I left you yesterday, and tell me everything."

As Lucetta helped her dress Meredith related the bewildering events, from discovering Emerson's troubling journal entry to the sudden explosion that had caused her to black out. She did not go into detail as to exactly what had happened between her and Alistair in his bed, or the nightmare and what he had told her about his affliction, but otherwise she freely admitted to confessing her feelings and encouraging his love making.

Lucetta remained silent as she adjusted the too-large sprigged muslin dress, pinning it at the waist and hem to keep her from tripping over the long skirts. By the time Meredith had finished recounting the events she stepped back and surveyed her with a narrow gaze.

"You are being very quiet," she told the older woman.

"I am trying to choose if I should accompany you to Starling House, go down the hall and shout very loudly at my employer, or find a large bottle of brandy and drink it. The brandy may win." Lucetta tapped her chin with a finger. "What troubles me most is the cause of all this: the fire. A hearth does not simply explode."

"Alistair found a glass shard on my face," Meredith said. "He believes someone dropped a lamp down the chimney in order to cause the fire. I am not so sure. Perhaps one of the workmen upstairs knocked it over, and did not realize where it fell."

"Only if he were working atop of the roof. There is no other access to the chimneys but there." Her cousin frowned. "I must relate this to Harshad, and we will investigate the cause. I will have him wake the colonel so he may accompany you."

"Please, don't," she begged. "Alistair has not been sleeping well since his return to England, and he needs to rest. I wish to speak to Mama and Papa before he does."

"You intend to be truthful with your parents about what has occurred between you and the colonel." When she nodded Lucetta sighed. "Given their expectations I imagine they will be very angry at first, but the news of your impending marriage may soften the blow."

Meredith grinned. "I am going to live here now, and be Alistair's wife. Would you ever have imagined that?"

"I am very happy for you, my dear." Her

cousin hugged her and kissed her cheek. "Now come. You will want some breakfast before you brace the family."

Meredith did not linger over the tea and scones Lucetta provided, for she knew her mother would be worried again over her absence. At least this would be the last time she would have to explain herself to her parents, for she knew Alistair would keep his promise. She expected he would obtain a special license so they could be married within a few days.

When Kshantu drove up to Starling House, Meredith didn't wait but climbed out herself and hurried inside. She expected at this early hour to find only the servants about their work, but Annie intercepted her on the way to the stairs and told her she should go to the sitting room. The maid wouldn't look at her at all, Meredith noticed.

Both of her parents stood as soon as she entered, and Lady Starling gave her a silent measuring look, her brows rising as she took in the borrowed gown.

"You never came home last night,

Daughter," Lord Starling said, sounding very stern.

"I did not." Looking at her father's dour expression made Meredith straighten. She would not cower anymore; she deserved a chance for a happy life. "I stayed over at Dredthorne Hall. I am in love with Colonel Thorne, Papa, and we are to marry."

The shrieked tirade she expected from her mother never came. Lady Starling simply nodded to her husband, who left the room without another word.

"Sit down, Meredith." Her mother waited until she did before she said, "You have disgraced yourself, and shamed this family to a degree that I never dreamed possible."

"I am in love, Mama," she repeated softly.

"You have returned home without your clothes, brazenly unrepentant, and baldly confessed to your licentious behavior. All of the servants have seen you. By this time tomorrow all of our friends and everyone in the village will know what you have done." Lady Starling came closer. "What do you have to say for yourself?"

She sighed. "Mama, I am marrying Alistair. I will be the mistress of Dredthorne Hall."

A beringed hand slapped Meredith's face so hard her teeth cut into the inside of her cheek.

"You are finished with Dredthorne Hall," Lady Starling snapped. "Your father and I forbid you to ever return to that place, or have anything to do with that disgusting man. We will send for Percival directly, and you will accept his offer of marriage. That may preserve what few shreds remain of your reputation."

Meredith touched her throbbing face, the taste of blood strong in her mouth. She had never seen her mother like this, but then she had never defied her so openly.

She has never seen me like this. We have become strangers to each other.

"No, I will not. If you send for my cousin, I will refuse him again. Spare him that humiliation, please." Slowly she rose to her feet. "We will talk about this when you have had time to calm yourself."

Leaving the sitting room, Meredith

walked past a gaping Annie in the hall and went upstairs to her bed chamber. She needed to pack for when Alistair would come to the manor, for she expected she would be leaving with him. She saw the jade silk dress, newly cleaned, hanging in her armoire, and took it out. Annie had somehow removed the boot blacking and repaired the tear with tiny, invisible stitches. Since it was the finest gown she possessed, it would serve as a wedding dress.

Meredith smiled as she imagined Alistair seeing her in it, and then helping her out of it.

She went to her dressing table and looked at her reflection in the mirror, which showed the livid marks of her mother's hand blazing against her pale skin. She touched the dark red patches, still unnerved by what had happened. Before today Lady Starling had never once lifted a hand to her. And why did she regard Alistair with such vehemence? She had been quite the reverse when Lucetta had first proposed they catalog the colonel's library.

In any event, Lucetta had been wrong. Nothing, it seemed, would soften this blow.

* * *

THORNE SLOWLY OPENED his eyes to see the afternoon sun streaming through the windows of his bed chamber. He sat up, still drowsy, and reached for his pocket watch. It assured him that he had slept most of the day away.

How long had it been since he had felt so replete? All thanks to the woman he loved.

He looked at the other half of his bed, and the small indentation on the pillow beside his own. A smile curved his mouth as he bent over to bury his face where Meredith had lain her head. The covering still smelled of her, and he breathed her in deeply. She had been everything to him in the night, friend and lover and consoler. Very soon she would be his wife, and he would share his bed with her every night.

Thorne didn't just feel like a new man. He felt like a different one. A man of hopes and dreams, not guilt and despair. Meredith had done that for him. It had started from the moment she had arrived in his life.

He dressed quickly but carefully, choosing a conservatively-cut dark green tail coat and black breeches. His cravat he tied simply but elegantly. When he faced the Starlings, he wanted to present the image of a son-in-law, not a dandy.

Emerging from his chamber, he took the stairs at a trot and followed the sound of Lucetta's voice where it came from his study. Some of the men were busy cleaning up the last traces of the fire, while she was peering carefully up inside the hearth.

"Miss Branwen."

"Colonel Thorne." She straightened and marched over to him. "Well, sir. You are still intent on marrying my cousin after last night's escapades, of which I have full knowledge, I might add?"

He grinned. "The moment she will have me."

"Good show. Then I will not shout at you or drink up all your brandy." She gestured toward the fireplace. "Harshad is up on the roof, inspecting the chimney for signs of tampering. In that bin there is what we removed from the ashes. Shattered lamp glass, and coals soaked with whale oil. You were correct about the fire being intentionally set."

"Is there anything you do not know?" he asked her gravely.

Lucetta thought for a moment. "As of this moment, who is responsible for these attempts to harm you and my cousin."

Thorne uttered a short, humorless laugh. "I think you mean Meredith."

"The fire was not started until you both occupied the study," his housekeeper told him. "The wood collapsed after you took my cousin into the tower. Since the evil work had to be done from a distance, I believe someone in this house is watching the two of you, and attacking when they know you are together."

What she said rang true to him, but for the motive. "What purpose would it serve to kill us both?"

"I don't think these attacks were meant to kill, only to harm." Lucetta looked over as Harshad entered the study. "What did you find above, Mr. Naveya?"

"Black boot marks on the side of the

chimney, Miss Branwen, and some broken shingling." The steward regarded Thorne. "A large brute with careless feet did this. Not one of us, Master."

No, his men would never be so clumsy, and all of them still wore brown calvary boots issued by their army. "None of the workmen I hired wear black boots." He glanced down at his own Hessians. "I do, however."

"I think we can rule you out as the perpetrator," Lucetta chided. "But I think it wise to perform a search of the house quickly. Someone may be hiding in one of the rooms, waiting for another opportunity to strike."

Thorne wanted to delegate the task to Harshad so he could go to Starling House to see Meredith. He expected Lord Starling would want reassurances about their engagement, and when to expect the wedding to occur. Lady Starling would likely want her pound of flesh before she consented. Yet in the back of his mind he could still see Meredith's skirts catching fire. Whoever had done this had to be stopped.

"Summon the men from the stables," he told his steward. "We will begin in the attics, and work our way down. I want a man on every stair case and terrace. Mind the rot. I want no more accidents in this house."

* * *

ANNIE LEFT a tray outside Meredith's door for luncheon, but otherwise no one came near her bed chamber. She readied her clothing and belongings for hasty removal in the event her parents ordered her to go, but as the hours dragged on, Alistair made no appearance. Tea time came and went and still no one came for her.

Had Lucetta neglected to mention that she had gone home? No, Alistair knew what she would be facing. Perhaps he expected her to come back to him. Meredith wasn't sure what to do but wait.

At last she decided she might try to talk to her father, who would have had enough time to calm down, and might be better persuaded to accept her decision. She put on a lavender dress, a color she knew Lord

Starling favored, and used a bit of rice powder to help cover the marks on her cheek. She would say nothing against her mother; that was the surest way to rekindled hostilities. Instead she would be forthright and adamant, but gently so.

Knowing the servants would be eager to eavesdrop, and anxious to avoid her mother, she took the back stairs down to the hall outside her father's book room, and went into the study adjoining it.

As a little girl Meredith had often hidden in the study, giggling when she heard her father's footsteps approaching. He had always scowled at her as he coaxed her from her hiding place to send her back to her nursemaid, but sometimes she would glance back and see him smiling faintly. He had never been openly affectionate, but he liked her more than her mother did.

Yes, her papa would listen to reason, she was sure of it.

Hearing her parents' voices from the other side, Meredith stood by the connecting door to listen. Even if she couldn't talk to her father just yet, perhaps she could find out why they objected to Alistair's proposal.

"–will do as he's told," her mother was saying. "He means to preserve the family honor. He's been trying very hard, you know."

"Percival is a simpleton," Lord Starling replied. "He is too busy preening to be of any use. Just as your sister is witless and useless."

Meredith winced. So much for her parents' adoration of her cousin and his mother.

"Our nephew is the future of the Starlings, my dear," his wife said soothingly. "Have patience. He may not be especially clever, but we can guide him along the path, just as your parents did."

"I swore to my parents that we would never allow a Thorne to keep his bride," her father said heavily, as if invoking a sacred oath. "Just as every generation has since Emerson Thorne stole Robert Starling's betrothed from him, and ruined our family."

"Yes, but Robert got his vengeance," Lady Starling said. "I often wonder how it might have been, had she married him instead of eloping with Thorne. The Starlings would never have been ruined. We would be living as we should, not scrimping and scraping on a pittance. Lettice Hardiwick would be begging for my cast-offs."

A cold knot formed in Meredith's middle as the words from Emerson Thorne's journal came back to her.

He took her from me, but I cannot prove it. I only know it in my heart, as surely as I know his rage at being denied his prize.

Alistair's ancestor had been writing about Robert Starling. If he had murdered Emerson's wife, and made his descendants carry on his terrible retribution... Icy horror filled her as she finally understood. Meredith's family was responsible for the Thorne curse.

"Now a Thorne means to wed our daughter," her father said, snarling the words. "I'll strangle her myself before I allow it."

"She will never marry him," Lady Starling scoffed. "No one will ever again be the mistress of Dredthorne Hall. My dear, don't you see the simplest solution? He is the last living member of his cursed family. We will see to it that the bloodline dies along with Alistair Thorne tonight."

Meredith clapped a hand over her mouth to stop herself from shrieking, and slowly backed away from the door. Turning on her heel, she fled.

Had her parents hired a killer to slip into Dredthorne Hall? Was he even now creeping up on Alistair? Her mother had said tonight, so there still might be time to warn her love.

She went out through the back of the house, intent on running to the stables to saddle a horse. Then she heard the sound of a wheels coming up the drive and rushed out to the front, where Percival appeared with his rig.

"Cousin, I am so glad to see you." She raced to his side. "Can you take me to Dredthorne Hall?"

He frowned at her. "Why should I do that?"

"Colonel Thorne is in terrible danger," Meredith told him as she climbed up beside him. "Really, Percival, it is a matter of life and death. We must go this instant."

"As you wish, Cousin." He tugged on the reins and headed back for the road. "I say, have you given any more thought to my offer?"

It took several hours, but Thorne and his men slowly searched each floor of the hall, stationing sentries as they checked every room, bath and closet from the attics to the ground level. Once they had ascertained that no one had hidden in any part of the house, he sent his men to search the stables, barn and other outbuildings while he met with Harshad and Lucetta in the front entry hall to discuss what they had found on the first floor.

"We found no trace," he told the housekeeper as he watched her take something from her pocket.

"I'm afraid we did." She extended a

blackened piece of metal. "I sifted through the ashes from the hearth in the study, and found it among some bits of glass."

The proof of who had caused the explosion confirmed Thorne's suspicions. "I must go to Starling House. Harshad, get the carriage."

The sound of one approaching made Lucetta go to the door. She glanced back at him. "It is Meredith, and Percival."

A moment later her cousin burst through the door and flung herself at Thorne. "Alistair, you must leave at once. I will go with you to the magistrate."

"She is very distraught," Percival said as he came in and closed the door. "She believes your life is in danger, Colonel. Something about a killer." He looked around the hall. "Where are your men?"

"They are out searching the property." Thorne stroked his hand over Meredith's wind-tousled hair before he put her at arm's length. "I must talk to the lieutenant now, my dear."

"There is no time for that, truly, Alistair." She gripped his sleeves. "I know why all these terrible things have happened."

"So do I." He eyed Percival as he placed the bit of metal in Meredith's hand. "It appears one of your medals is missing, Lieutenant. The one denoting valor in battle, I believe."

Her cousin tucked in his chin to examine his jacket front. "Egad, I think you are right." He touched a torn ribbon. "I will have to obtain a replacement straight away."

"No need. I found it in the hearth in the colonel's study," Lucetta told him. "I imagine it fell off while you were on the roof, dropping that lamp down the chimney. Just as you scuffed your boots against it."

Percival's expression went from puzzled to guarded. "Don't know what you mean, Cousin."

"I don't understand," Meredith said slowly, staring at the broken medal before gazing at him. "Why would you do such a thing?"

"He knew we were together in the study," Thorne said. "Just as he knew when we entered the staircase tower. He has been hiding in the house and spying on us. He was jealous."

Percival folded his arms. "That is nonsense."

"I daresay it's not the first time he's tried to hurt you, Meredith." Thorne walked over to the lieutenant, close enough to make him take a step back. "In the crowd at the ball he might have easily tripped you. Sabotaging your rig so that it would come apart also would prove simple. When he found the overturned rig and realized you had been rescued, he smashed it to hide what he had done. How many other times have you caused Meredith to suffer mishaps, I wonder? Dozens of times? Every time?"

A cunning look came over the lieutenant's face. "You can't prove any of that."

Lucetta slowly shook her head. "Oh, Percival."

Thorne drew back his fist and punched him squarely in the face, sending him staggering backward.

Meredith clenched her hand around the medal. "You did these things to me on purpose, Cousin? You arranged all these accidents?"

"I did nothing of the sort. The colonel is obviously mistaken." He wiped his bloody nose on his sleeve. "I would never harm you, Meredith. You know that. I want to marry you."

She glanced at Thorne. "My death would bring him nothing. The estate is entailed, and when my parents die Percival will inherit everything. He has no reason to want me dead."

"I don't believe he wished to kill you. He did these things to create chances to rescue you," Thorne said. "What he desired was the admiration he received each time he came to save you from some terrible mishap."

"He is deceiving you, Cousin," Percival insisted. "I adore you; you know that. How many times have I come to your aid? Remember the poacher's trap? I freed you from that terrible contraption."

"That may have been the only time he genuinely rescued you," Thorne told Meredith. "As a child I expect he would have been overly praised for his heroics."

"My parents did make much of it," she murmured.

"Some people become so gratified by such acclaim that earning more consumes them. I have seen many such men in the Army, who will charge recklessly into great danger, all for the chance at glory." He gestured at the lieutenant's heavily-decorated jacket. "Yet I doubt he was awarded any of those medals. He probably purchased them or stole them from their true owners."

"You are the jealous one, Thorne," Percival said, sneering at him. "She will be my wife. She has always been mine."

A terrible calm came over Meredith's face.

"It *was* you, all these years. Admit it to me." She threw the medal at his head and shouted, "Tell me the truth."

"I have made some mistakes in the past, Cousin." He wiped at his bloody nose. "Only when we were nippers. As I grew older, I saw the error of my ways. I joined the military."

"That is why I had no mishaps while you were gone," Meredith said dully. "You were not here to cause them. You were too far away to hurt me."

"Did someone discover what you were doing to your cousin?" Thorne asked. "Your mother, perhaps? Did she insist you take that commission, not only to send you away, but to protect Meredith from you?" When Percival blustered, he added, "Do you think Lavinia will lie for you again, Starling?"

"That is why Aunt does not want you to marry me." Meredith looked sick. "She knew what you had done. What you would keep doing."

"Meredith, please." Percival reached out to her. "Thorne can never understand how much affection we have for each other. Did I not offer you my heart? How could I ask you to be my wife if I–" Percival's head rocked back as her hand slapped his cheek.

"Do you have any notion of what you have done?" As he gaped at her, she slapped him again. "You have torn my flesh and burned my limbs and broken my bones, over and over. You have terrified me and scarred me and filled my life with pain and despair." She almost hit him a third time, but she could not bear to touch him again.

"You don't understand." Tears filled Percival's eyes as his lower lip trembled. "I am a Starling."

"You are a monster," Lucetta said softly.

"We will let the magistrate decide what to do with him." Thorne put his arm around Meredith's shoulders. "Come away now. We have much to discuss."

The loud crack of gunfire made him whirl, and he saw Lucetta stiffen and look down at the spreading, wet red stain on her gown. As she sank to the floor, Harshad shouted and rushed to her, and then was flung backward as Percival shot him. With a cry Meredith dropped down beside the housekeeper, gathering handfuls of her skirt and pressing it against the wound.

Thorne rushed at Percival, stopping short as the lieutenant produced another double-barreled flintlock and aimed it at Meredith.

"I told you, she is mine," Percival said, smiling. "And if I cannot marry her, well, then, no one will."

The door opened behind him, and Lord

and Lady Starling came to stand beside their nephew.

"Well, my dear," Meredith's mother said. "It is a good thing that you brought two pistols."

As Percival's gaze shifted Thorne lunged at him, shoving him into the Starlings and sending the three of them sprawling. He then seized Meredith by the arm and dragged her to her feet. "Run."

MEREDITH DRAGGED her skirts up with both hands as she ran with Thorne into the sitting room and through the second ballroom into a small storage room. That led to the arch to the staircase tower opposite the one that had been sealed off for repairs. There he ducked under the stairs to try the door that led outside, only to find it locked.

"Up," he said to her.

As they climbed Meredith heard Percival shouting for her, his voice growing closer. "Leave me behind, and hide," she told him, tugging at his arm. "They won't hurt me."

"I am never leaving you again," Thorne told her, and led her up another flight until they reached the third floor. There he led her through the arch and out toward the servants' quarters. He stopped by a table filled with the carpenter's hand tools and some bricks they had removed from one of the hearths. "We'll lure them up here, then return to the first floor and take Lucetta and Harshad into the hidden library."

Meredith was almost sure her cousin and the steward were dying, if not dead. Percival likely knew every hiding spot in the hall. She looked down at the blood on her hands, and then at the landing in front of the staircase tower. She knew of only one way to end this feud forever and picked up a brick.

Could she do this, to save Alistair? They were her family. He was the man she loved.

"I love you," she said as she put her arms around him.

Thorne kissed her. "We will survive this night, I promise you."

She nodded, and then hit him with the

brick. He gave her a single, stunned look before he fell to the floor.

Moving Thorne took all of her strength, but she managed to drag him over and prop him against the wall by the landing. She knelt down, smearing his brow and face with Lucetta's blood before she did the same to one of the carpenter's hammers. She then stepped carefully to one side of Thorne, keeping to the part of the flooring that had already been replaced.

Percival and her parents emerged from opposite the staircase tower. Her cousin pointed his pistol at her as they approached, lowering it when he saw how she was standing over Thorne. "Meredith?"

"He was so angry. He said he was going to have all of you put in prison," she told him, letting the tears spill down her face. "I couldn't let him do that, so I hit him. I think I've killed him, Papa."

"The last of the Thornes, dead by my daughter's hand." Her father sounded half-gloating, half-proud.

"You see? It is just as you told me. She is a Starling." Percival put his arm around Lady Starling, who was smiling.

"We must make it look as if he fell," Meredith said, and made a show of trying to move Thorne. "I will need all of you to help, please."

Her parents and cousin hurried over, stepping onto the landing as they reached for Thorne. Meredith closed her eyes as she heard the rotted wood give way, and the terrible screams as all three plunged through a cloud of wood dust and debris.

She allowed herself a moment to sob against Alistair's shoulder, and then leaned out to look through the hole in the landing. Three floors down the twisted bodies atop the pile of new rubble did not move.

Thorne stirred, and then opened his eyes. "Meredith?"

"I've broken the curse, Alistair," she told him wearily. "Both of them."

A WEEK after the collapse at Dredthorne Hall, Meredith helped her aunt walk from the churchyard to her carriage, where they stood for a long moment looking back at the three new graves bedecked with flowers. Some mourners from the funeral still lingered; Lady Hardiwick seemed especially grief-stricken. Beside her Prudence eyed the vicar's curate and pretend to cough into a handkerchief to cover her giggles.

Most of those who had attended had murmured their condolences to Meredith, who graciously accepted them when she wanted to shriek at them for being so blind.

"After you refused him, Lettice had hopes that Percival would take that simpering miss off her hands," Lavinia murmured. "Lucky for her he lost his footing."

Alistair Thorne had insisted on reporting the deaths of Meredith's cousin and parents as a tragic accident, and the shootings of Lucetta and Harshad as accidental. No one questioned this, thanks to corroborating statements from two of the victims and Meredith herself. So many deaths spurred a new crop of rumors in the village about Dredthorne Hall, which was now considered haunted as well as cursed.

Meredith helped her aunt into the

carriage. "I will see you back at the house tonight, Aunt."

"You're a good girl to look after me, but I have decided to leave." She patted her hand. "I will be leaving tomorrow for Scotland. I have an old friend there who wishes a companion, and she has a nice little cottage. I have no more reason to stay in Renwick."

Watching the carriage roll off, Meredith felt a fresh wave of sorrow. She hadn't told Lavinia the truth of what had happened, but she suspected she knew any way. She would always be grateful to her for trying to protect her from her son and his ghastly need to inflict pain for his own glory.

Now if she could only rid herself of the dark legacy her parents had left to her.

From the church Meredith walked over to the parsonage, where she called on Mrs. Branwen. Deidre invited her to dinner, but Meredith asked if she might simply visit with their guest. She found Lucetta swathed in blankets but busy with her embroidery.

"Have you come to rescue me?" her cousin demanded. "For if I stitch one more posy I think I will tear out my hair and run amok."

"You may not run anywhere until your wound has healed," the vicar's wife chided as she brought in a tray of tea and biscuits.

"How many posies have you stitched this week?" Lucetta countered.

"Once you are healed your life will be far more interesting. Your fiancé wishes to have the wedding as soon as we may, which dear Jeffrey says we must hold here." She smiled at Meredith. "It is to be Christian and Hindu. I am making her dress. It is beautiful."

"I am a housekeeper. My good rose linen is perfectly suited for a wedding." Lucetta glared at her sister-in-law. "You should not go to so much trouble for me. I am old. So is Harshad."

"You are getting married." Deidre leaned over to kiss the top of her head. "You would look lovely in a potato sack, but I am making you a dress. I am much more skilled at sewing than cooking, so stop grumbling and thank me."

Lucetta smiled up at her. "Thank you, Sister."

They chatted about the wedding plans until Mrs. Branwen excused herself to check on a stew she was making.

Meredith put down her tea cup and regarded her cousin. "My aunt goes to Scotland tomorrow. Since your brother is the only male heir the attorneys can find, Starling House and the estate goes to him."

"He will never live there," Lucetta said, grimacing. "He and Deidre are happiest here, in their little parsonage. Have you been to see Alistair?"

"Not since I spoke with the magistrate. There has been so much to do with the funerals, and helping Aunt Lavinia." Meredith plucked at her skirt. "And there is that other matter, when I bashed him in the head with a brick before I killed my family."

"Nonsense. They killed themselves. You saved our lives," Lucetta told her firmly. "Now go to Dredthorne and talk to Alistair, and do try to keep your clothes on while you do. All that can wait until after you are married. At least, that is what I tell myself and Harshad."

Meredith chuckled, but as she left the parsonage a short time later her amusement settled into a solid lump in her stomach. She had been avoiding Alistair, and Dredthorne, as she did not know what to say to him. The Starlings had spent generations tormenting and murdering the Thornes. Her own parents had planned to kill him. How could a man love a woman so tainted by her own family?

Yet she could not stop thinking about Alistair Thorne. Every night she lay in her lonely bed wishing he was beside her. She worried his nightmares had returned, or he had taken to avoiding sleep again. Her body ached for his touch. Her heart wrenched with shame over the terrible cruelties the Starlings had inflicted. She felt pulled in two directions, one toward him, the other away.

"Good afternoon, Miss Starling."

Even now she could hear him in her head. "Oh, go away."

A shadow crossed her path. "If you truly wish me to, I will."

Meredith looked up into Thorne's face and laughed a little. "Forgive me. I thought I imagined you."

"I could say the same." He offered her his arm. "Come and take a drive with me."

She could see Kshantu waiting with his carriage a short distance away. "Have you been following me?"

"Waiting for you," he corrected as he guided her to the carriage, and helped her in. "I thought it best that I not call at the house. Your aunt is recovering?"

Meredith told him about Lavinia and her decision to move to Scotland, and Starling House going to Jeffrey Branwen. She mentioned how well Lucetta looked, and inquired after Harshad, whom Thorne told her had improved enough to leave his bed for short periods to join in the meals with the men and survey the ongoing restoration work.

Everyone was getting better, it seemed, except her.

As they approached the lionsgate at Dredthorne Meredith braced herself for a wave of dread. She had not been back to the hall since that night, and she wondered if she would feel like a murderess as she stepped into the front hall.

"I considered attending the services

today, but I did not wish to cause a stir," Thorne told her as he led her into the sitting room. "Should I ring for tea, or did the vicar's wife attend to that?"

Meredith went and closed the door before she faced him. "Please stop being so polite. We are alone. You may say whatever you wish to me."

"Such as, 'You hit me in the head with a brick' or 'You saved my life?'" He started toward her. "You did both."

"Alistair.' She put her hand on his chest to stop him from gathering her into his arms. "You know what I mean. I am a Starling. You are a Thorne. My family… All I can say is I am so sorry for what they did to yours. I never knew."

"What of how they treated you? Your parents wished you to marry your cousin, the monster, and kill me, the man you love." He trailed his fingers along her cheek. "Meredith, my dearest love, without you I would be dead. So would Lucetta and Harshad, I believe. You made a terrible choice to stop three killers, and save three lives."

"Your men were able to help my cousin

and your steward." She turned her face away. "I am the killer now. Perhaps that was meant to be. I am their daughter."

"Only if you continue their wretched legacy." He took her hands in his. "Or you could choose another name. Join my family. Marry me. Become a Thorne. Let the Starlings rest in peace. No one ever need know about the truth behind the curse. When our time comes, you and I will take it to our graves."

Meredith stared at him. "You would want that, after all they've done to hurt you?"

"I want you." He bent his head to hers, and brushed his mouth against her lips. "Say yes, Meredith. Be my wife. Be a Thorne."

Her eyelids drooped, and her skin began tingling all over. "If I say yes, what will happen?"

"Let me think." Thorne pressed her back against the door with the weight of his body. "You will make me very happy. I will pick you up in my arms, and carry you to my bed chamber." He kissed her again.

When his mouth lifted she gasped, "And then?"

"I will ravish you thoroughly so that you cannot change your mind." He nipped her earlobe before he murmured, "Very, very thoroughly. Deeply. Repeatedly."

Meredith could feel the hard length of him now against her belly. "Alistair, you are making it very difficult for me to think. What I mean to say is, will we stay here, at Dredthorne Hall?"

He drew back and studied her face. "Do you wish to?"

"My parents died here," she reminded him softly. "As much as I love this house, no, I cannot stay here. I want to make a home that is ours, in a place that has never been cursed or filled with torment or terrible secrets. A house where we may build a new legend together. One of happiness."

Thorne nodded. "I agree."

"Then I will marry you, Alistair." Meredith felt the last of the shadows melt away inside her. Here was her lovely, golden-haired, blue-eyed prince, the man of her dreams, and she could have him for the rest of her life. "Take me to your bed chamber, sir."

True to his word he scooped her off her feet and carried her up the steps. Along the way they passed Harshad, who grinned and nodded to her as he carefully made his way down the stairs. Meredith laughed as Thorne kicked open his door and rushed to the bed, and dropped her atop the coverlet. A moment later he was on top of her, his clever hands holding her face as he kissed her breathless.

For a moment Meredith felt as if her heart might burst. Then Thorne rolled to his side, pulling her onto hers.

"I have wanted you so much in my bed, I dreamed of it," he told her as he began unbuttoning her gown. "I woke up, not in terror, but hard and hot and ready to have you."

"I am sorry I was not here to provide you with me," she murmured, and glanced down as he worked her bodice down to her waist. "Alistair, you are making me dreadfully needy. I wish you were inside me right now."

Thorne pushed her onto her back,

heaved up her skirts, jerked down her drawers and opened the flap of his breeches.

"I remember that formidable weapon," Meredith teased as he tugged out his rigid shaft. "Give that to me this instant, sir."

"You are greedy," he muttered as he guided himself to the wet, clenching gates of her sex. "I like that very much about you."

They both groaned as he worked himself into her, his cock so hard it made her gush in response. Slowly he sank deep, filling and stretching her, until he completed their joining and looked down at her.

"You make me so happy," she told him.

"I love you, Meredith Thorne," he said, and began to move inside her with slow, long strokes. "I think I have since the moment you sprawled at my feet. I thought about ravishing you the moment I brought you inside. Now I think I should have, but for my men."

"I would have made a great deal of maidenly noise," she mentioned. "They would have guessed."

What he did to her with his lovely, thick cock made her breasts swell and her nipples tighten, until Meredith gripped his hand and brought it to her, rubbing their fingers over her aching mounds. He watched, his eyes narrow and hot, before he seized her hips and thrust powerfully into her, determined, demanding.

Meredith knew what he was doing. He was claiming her, fucking her, making her as thoroughly his as he had promised. She could feel her own pleasure building around his hard strokes, her nub pulsing madly, and the increase in heat and swelling that told her he was close to pumping her full of his seed. She loved that moment. She loved everything about making love with Alistair.

She knew what to say to him as she trembled on the very brink of it. "Make me with child, my love. Give me your baby now."

Thorne brought her hand to his mouth, biting her palm as he drove deep, flinging her into the hot, sweet pleasure of release, as he jetted into her, working every creamy spurt deep into her core.

They collapsed, and Meredith held him, their clothes a tangle, their bodies shaking with the force of their bliss. For a time, it was all she could do to breathe, and feel him, and know that the love she had wanted so badly had finally found her, and taken her, and would keep her heart safe.

CHAPTER 12

In the dining room Harshad sat down gingerly next to his new wife, still not convinced he should take this place at the master's table. He smiled at Meredith, who was untying a large scroll, and then eyed Thorne.

"My wife has a proposal for the two of you," Thorne said as she spread out the drawing of a large house nestled among gardens and fruit trees. "We are thinking of purchasing this property."

"It is a little larger than Dredthorne," Meredith told them, "but the house is perfectly suitable for a family, and the grounds are beautiful. The previous owners took their staff with them, so we will need to hire servants and gardeners and groundskeepers, and manage the dozen or so tenant farms. Oh, and there are apple and plum orchards that are quite productive. In all we think about fifty new hires, since Alistair's men will be busy working with him on our horse-breeding venture."

"I see." Lucetta peered at the drawing. "What is that little manor there behind the great house? A dowager's house?"

"It was, I believe," Thorne said. "It will be your home, should you wish to come with us."

Harshad frowned. "We do not need a house of our own, Master."

"I am a housekeeper," Lucetta put in. "I will be busy keeping your house."

"Not if you agree to accept new positions in our household," Meredith said. "Harshad, Alistair would like you and Lucetta to be our estate managers. Our partners in our business ventures. You would each have a percentage of the profits along with a salary."

Lucetta's eyes widened. "That is quite generous."

"You will earn it. You will have the responsibility of overseeing the property and the staff, as well as our financials," Thorne said. "Meredith and I will work with you as we make improvements to the house, hire new staff, and expand our investments. We will rely on your advice to plan our future."

"I see." Lucetta looked at her husband before she said, "What will become of Dredthorne Hall?"

"We will be continuing the repairs and renovations while we arrange to lease the property," Meredith said. "It will be another of our investment ventures."

"And if we wish not to go with you?" Harshad asked.

"Then we will leave you to look after Starling House for Mr. Branwen." Thorne smiled. "I believe he has already spoken to you about the possibility, Lucetta."

"Yes, he has." She contemplated the drawing again before she regarded her husband. "Well, my dear, if you are in agreement with this scheme, I would like to go with the Thornes." She eyed Meredith. "With the understanding that I will need time next fall when we are so blessed to increase our family."

Harshad grinned. "We are having a baby. She will not say that."

Meredith took hold of Thorne's hand. "What a coincidence. So are we."

"Well." Her cousin took hold of her husband's dark hand. "I daresay our children will grow up together at the new estate. Have you decided on a name for the house, Alistair?"

"Meredith and I have been arguing about it incessantly," he assured her. "I think Thornhill has a strong ring to it."

"So does bramble patch," his wife said drily. "I wished for Merryweather."

"Call the place Christmas House and be done with it," Thorne drawled.

Lucetta eyed the bowl of roses in the center of the table. "What do you think of Rosethorne? It has rather a nice poetic ring to it. Speaks to life and love. The sweet and the prickly. And we are all rising to begin anew."

Thorne exchange a look with Meredith before he smiled and nodded. "It is perfect."

* * *

AFTER DINNER THORNE stood with his wife in the reception room as they watched the first snow falling, carpeting the grounds around the hall in pure, glittering white. She shivered and pressed against his side, her hand slipping under his lapel to idly caress his hard chest.

"More of that, Mrs. Thorne, and you are for the bed chamber," he warned her sternly.

"I am always for the bed chamber," she chided, and then sighed. "So, we must leave tomorrow, and I think we will not be returning. It is a good feeling, but sad, too. How do you feel about that, Mr. Thorne?"

"Happy. Relieved." He rested his cheek against the top of her head. "Ready."

As they walked past the painted outer wall of the dining room, Meredith stopped and looked up at him. "What of Emerson's journals? Harshad never had the chance to remove them from the cases. Do we dare to leave them behind?"

"I think we must." Thorne watched her

frown. "We can replace the children's books to conceal the cache. As you said, only we will know they are there."

"Perhaps it is best to leave some of Dredthorne's secrets for others to delve." She tucked her arm through his. "And you may make me very unhappy, and I will leave you and return here to wallow in my misery over our broken marriage. I will need something to read."

"You will never leave me," Thorne predicted. "But I might leave you."

"Then I will know where to find you, and what you are reading." She tugged him away from the wall. "Come along. You must make good on your threat to ravish me a dozen times a day. I am keeping count, you know."

He kissed her temple. "I am never leaving you."

* * *

A WEEK after the Thornes and the Naveyas departed Renwick for their new home in the west, Dredthorne Hall stood empty, wrapped in a thick cloak of winter white. Frost had crept up the windows, furring some of the panes and etching glittering scrolls across others. Within its cold walls the hearths stood empty, and the furnishings draped in dust cloths. Behind the Pandora panel in the dining room the hidden library once more lay concealed, its cache of secrets hidden behind rows of children's books.

Night fell, and day rose. In the darkness creatures that crept near the hall sniffed at its doors and windows before slinking away. After dawn, sunshine poured over the soot-stained chimneys and ice-coated roof tiles, melting the lightest layers, and causing cracks in the thick white beneath them. Birds, now gone south to warmer climes, no longer brightened the air with their songs. The estate seemed enchanted, and asleep, as if trapped by some fairytale curse.

Yet on this day horse-drawn carts creaked slowly along the drive, each filled with wood and plaster and boxes of tools, driven by men with weathered faces and shrewd eyes. More men followed the carts in wagons, their homespun garments rough, their hands shiny with calluses. They gathered in front of the hall in a loose, uneasy group. Mutters about the place were traded, outlandishly embellished and cuttingly simple.

Three people had fallen to their deaths here less than a month past. Everyone needed work, no one particularly wanted this job.

"Right then. We're to finish the flooring on the third, and then begin the tower." The carpenter Thorne had hired as his foreman gestured to the other men. "We've got a pile of work, lads, let's get on with it."

As the men reluctantly retrieved their tools and supplies to carry them inside, a few looked up at the dark windows above them. From their angle it seemed as if the house had eyes fixed on them. One of the more religious men made the sign of a cross over himself. Others thought longingly of home, and family, and whiskey, or anything that would keep them from looking into those huge black eyes.

Dredthorne Hall remained as it had always been, silently watching them.

THE END

• • • • •

Another adventure awaits you in *Mistress of Darkness (Dredthorne Hall Book 2)*

For a sneak peek, turn the page.

Mistress of Secrets (Dredthorne Hall Book 2)

Excerpt

CHAPTER ONE

Nothing had ever been good enough for Regina; not even her fiancée. As Gwen listened to the soft clapping of the horse's hooves against the packed snow, she reviewed her sister's cryptic letter again. Its meaning was clear, even if it was lacking in the thousand specifics Gwen would have liked: Regina had run away from home. Her betrayal still carried a razor edge of pain. Her sister had run away mere weeks before the elaborate wedding that Gwen and her mother had spent months planning, preparing, and slaving over. She wasn't merely thoughtless. Regina was *ungrateful*. Gwen would have done anything for the beautiful, white-and-crystalline celebration that she and her mother had devoted so many countless hours to making possible.

"Regina, where are you?" she whispered into the growing country darkness.

The crisp air, with a few gently pirouetting snowflakes, made the jingling of the halter sing all the clearer in Gwen's ears. The sound reminded her not of Christmas, but of the tiny, sparkling bells that they had imported from Paris specifically for her absent sister's nuptials. Gwen had been looking forward, with a tinge of jealousy, to the sound of so many bells ringing while Regina and Christopher walked down the aisle. Now, all that Gwen had to look forward to was the dread responsibility of her current mission. Gwen, older and only sister, now carried the weight of telling poor Christopher that his willful bride had become wayward.

Gwen sighed, closing her eyes, trusting the horse to do its work. The loss of her sister was almost too much for her to bear. Regina had been a constant presence in Gwen's life, and she had never thought that they would be apart. They would marry and live in the same town, see each other every Sunday for dinner, raise their children together...

I do not know who I am anymore, Regina had written in a wobbly script. *But I know that I cannot be with Christopher, not now. Perhaps not ever.*

If there was a hideous truth behind her words, Regina's parting message did not specify it. Gwen's own letter to Christopher avoided telling him any of the dire news.

Please, meet me, sir. I need to speak with you about my sister and my family as soon as can be arranged.

Gwen's note was enigmatic, perhaps, but it wouldn't be right to tell Christopher the crushing news in any other way than in person. She had at least been able to summon that much courage.

She peered ahead and spied Dredthorne Hall looming in the distance. The house was foreboding, a large harbinger of doom, if the rumors from town were to be believed. Gwen knew some of the details of the place already. It was of overwhelming size, with fifty-eight rooms and four floors, and was one of the oldest halls in the region. Gwen spared a thought for the poor staff that would have to keep the house. It reminded her of an aged lady of class and manners who had once been beautiful in her prime. While the overarching structure was still there, the details were fading into the background, overwhelmed by time, decay, and inevitability.

How the Sheratons came to own it or what exactly they planned to do with the place was less clear to Gwen. She had avoided the family prior to the engagement due to the poor manners of Christopher's older brother, Robert. She hoped that her mission to Christopher could be completed without having to deal with that ogre. It was fortunate that Regina had found a match with such a worthy family, but that did not mean Gwen had to like her new brother-in-law. Her mind hurried to correct the detail: the man who could have become a brother-in-law had Regina not vanished into the night with little more than a crumpled piece of paper left behind.

The rig rolled past the gate, the gentle beat of hooves on snow being replaced by the clack against brick. Stately twin lions carved from Italian marble sat atop pedestal columns and seemed to gaze down on her in disapproval. Gray slate roofs capped the soft buff stone of the house. Two towers flanked it, as though it were a small castle. The closer she got, the higher its weathered facade rose, along with her anxiety. Gwen took a deep breath as she slowed the rig to a stop. She was up to this task, she assured herself, for she had to be. There was simply no escape from it, short of finding her lost sister.

A footman approached and held out his hand to help her. She took it, lifting her dress as she stepped down, and it took everything in her to keep her face agreeable at the sight that greeted her. In that moment, she desperately wished that her home was close enough to Dredthorne Hall for her to return this evening, but *nothing* was close to Dredthorne Hall.

Robert Sheraton, Christopher's elder

brother, stood tall in the midst of a small army of servants, with no Christopher in sight. The older brother's dark hair and eyes matched his somber dress. He wore a white shirt, cravat, and waist coat, accompanied by a black jacket and trousers.

Gwen had the prudence to withhold the groan that he inspired. There was nothing about Robert that appealed to her. He was prickly, quick to speak his anger, easy to enrage, and condescending. Robert made friends with no one, and had always seemed to prefer it that way. She watched as he tucked a strand of black hair behind his ear and his movement reminded her of her own appearance. She smoothed her skirts and tried to stand taller as she approached him.

Hiding her displeasure as best she could, as she had been trained, Gwen said, "Mr. Sheraton, to what do I owe this pleasure?"

With satisfaction, she noted that she had managed to sound the perfect picture of politeness. If Robert could find anything disagreeable in their meeting, it would not be her words.

He cleared his throat, smoothing a

minuscule wrinkle along his coat, and bowed slightly.

"Miss Archer. How wonderful to see you," he said with a deep voice that was suited to his large frame. But she wondered if anything he spoke besides her name was true, remembering their last encounter, in her youth. "My brother has not yet arrived from London. He asked that you remain here to await his presence in order to personally receive your....*news*."

• • • • •

Buy *Mistress of Darkness (Dredthorne Hall Book 2)*

For Mr. H.

9 781950 575169